"Adel's happy today."

"She's always happy but more so since I brought her home," Faith said.

Josiah took a bite of sandwich. "Why do you think that is?"

She shrugged. "Who knows? Maybe it's because she knows this farm is ours. Maybe it's because you gave her a horse."

She tossed a half-exasperated look in his direction and he laughed.

"She has Hope's eyes. Pale blue, like a robin's egg," he said.

She jerked and blinked at him. "That's an odd thing to say."

"Not really. You two were identical, but I could always tell you apart just by looking at your eyes. Other than that, Adel looks just like you."

She glanced down, her sandwich forgotten. "I…I suppose so."

They were quiet a moment, both l_____ _ _heir own thoughts. The trickling of t'_____ rustling of the trees over'_____ _as a beautiful, id_____ Josiah could almos_____ That they all belon_

Then reality in

Leigh Bale is a *Publishers Weekly* bestselling author. She is the winner of the prestigious Golden Heart® Award and was a finalist for the Gayle Wilson Award of Excellence and the Booksellers' Best Award. The daughter of a retired US forest ranger, she holds a BA in history. Married in 1981 to the love of her life, Leigh and her professor husband have two children and two grandkids. You can reach her at leighbale.com.

Books by Leigh Bale

Love Inspired

Secret Amish Babies

The Midwife's Christmas Wish
Her Forbidden Amish Child
An Amish Christmas Wish
Her Hidden Amish Child

Colorado Amish Courtships

Runaway Amish Bride
His Amish Choice
Her Amish Christmas Choice
Healing Their Amish Hearts
Her Amish Chaperone

Men of Wildfire

Her Firefighter Hero
Wildfire Sweethearts
Reunited by a Secret Child

Visit the Author Profile page at LoveInspired.com for more titles.

Her Hidden
Amish Child

Leigh Bale

LOVE INSPIRED
INSPIRATIONAL ROMANCE

LOVE INSPIRED®

INSPIRATIONAL ROMANCE

Recycling programs
for this product may
not exist in your area.

ISBN-13: 978-1-335-59685-7

Her Hidden Amish Child

For questions and comments about the quality of this book, please contact us at CustomerService@Harlequin.com.

Love Inspired
22 Adelaide St. West, 41st Floor
Toronto, Ontario M5H 4E3, Canada
www.LoveInspired.com

Printed in U.S.A.

But seek ye first the kingdom of God,
and his righteousness; and all these things
shall be added unto you.
—*Matthew* 6:33

For my beloved Jared, Amy, Makiah and Ellie Jo. You have increased our family with joy and made our lives whole.

Chapter One

She could do this. She was an intelligent, thinking woman, and she'd done it zillions of times before.

Standing in the enclosed back porch of her great-aunt's early-1900s farmhouse, Faith Mast gazed at the postwar-era washer with open hostility. The machine had a simple design, easily adapted to the rumbling diesel generator sitting outside on the wooden deck. As a devout Amish woman, Faith never used electricity. Having been raised in this house by their great-aunt and uncle, Faith and her identical twin sister, Hope, had learned to wash clothes on this device. But ever since Faith got her hand caught between the rollers and broke two fingers, she'd hated this washer so much that she'd named it *der umensch*.

The monster.

Flipping open the lid, she peered inside. Like the rinse tub resting nearby, it was clean as a whistle. Faith expected nothing less from her great-aunt Fern. The elderly woman had been a meticulous cook, gardener and housekeeper. The perfect Amish farmer's wife, except for one thing. Aunt Fern had never been able to have a child of her own. Instead, she and her husband had taken Faith and Hope into their home when they were barely five years old, after their parents died in a tragic buggy accident. Faith's aunt, uncle and sister were all gone now. And she missed them more than she could say.

Reaching for the water hoses, she laid the open ends inside the washing tub and snapped the agitator into place. While the basin filled, she gazed out the wide window at the warm April day. She'd been gone just shy of four years. The last time she was here, the back lawn had been verdant green. Colorful pansies, marigolds and petunias had filled the flower beds. Barley and alfalfa had flourished in her uncle's open fields. Now the grass and flowers were dead and the white frame house needed painting...both inside and out.

To the south, the apple orchard was starting to leaf out with bright pinkish-white blossoms. Soon, the trees would be covered with red-and-yellow delicious apples needing to be picked. Faith's mouth watered at the thought of biting into one. But she wouldn't be here in the fall when the fruit matured. It had been so difficult to leave and even more challenging to return. But the hardest thing she'd ever done was turn her back on Josiah Brenneman, the love of her life.

Glancing down, she saw the tub was a quarter full of water. Reaching for a bucket sitting on the middle shelf, she added shavings of homemade soap. Aunt Fern had taught her to make the stuff and she quite enjoyed the task. Since the bucket was almost empty, Faith resolved to make more later in the week. She could buy detergent from the store in town but it seemed too much of a betrayal to her aunt's memory.

And just like that, Faith's eyes burned with tears. How she missed her aunt and uncle. How she missed her sister. But her Amish upbringing had taught her not to cry over the deaths of loved ones. They were in *Gott*'s care now and her tears would never bring them back. But oh, how she hated being alone in the world.

Correction. She still had Adel, her sister's three-year-old daughter. And the little girl needed her now more than ever. Because she was all alone in the world, too.

Shaking off her gloomy thoughts, Faith reached for the pile of clothes she'd laid on the floor a few minutes earlier. She pressed the dark dresses and stockings into the sudsy water until they were completely submerged. Once she got these washed, she'd start painting the house. If she wanted to sell the farm, she'd need to spruce up the place. With her uncle being gone over six years, she had a long to-do list. On her own, it would take months to get it all done. Obviously, Aunt Fern had been struggling to keep up with the tasks. And that made Faith feel guilty. She should have been here. But considering Hope's situation, that had been impossible. If Faith wanted to sell the place and get out of here anytime soon, she'd need to hire someone to assist with the chores.

But who?

While the agitator did its work, she went outside and hauled a ladder from the outside shed over to the front porch. The two-story white frame house she'd loved was now covered with peeling paint. It'd take a lot of work to remedy that, but she could do it. The early spring weather was nice and warm. Ideal for painting.

She unpackaged the brushes and rollers she'd purchased yesterday in town. The farming community of Riverton, Colorado, had a sparse population of no more than five thousand people. Thankfully, it still had a building supply store. During the three days since Faith's return, she'd already scrubbed the small bathroom, spacious kitchen and bedrooms to a shine. Now it was time to roll up her sleeves and do the heavier jobs.

A quick check of the laundry told her she needed to squeeze out the load. Flipping on the wringer switch, she lifted the soggy pieces of cloth out of the sudsy water. Between the low drone of the generator outside and the rattling machine inside, she could barely hear herself think. The racket might awaken little Adel from her afternoon nap, but it couldn't be helped.

One by one, Faith fed the clothes through the wringer. At one point, she adjusted the fabric so it didn't ride too close to the gears, which would put an ugly streak of grease across the clothes. When she returned to Akron, Ohio, she'd buy a small house for her and Adel to live in, complete with an automatic washing machine. She'd gladly pay one of the Amish men in her cousin's congregation to adapt the washer to diesel power. Then she'd have no more wringers. No more pinched fingers.

She leaned over the wringer cap and peered at the opposite side to ensure the dresses were falling into the rinse tub like they should. A sudden jerk pulled her chest close against the tub. A cry of alarm burst from her lips and a blaze of panic scorched her throat. She tried to pull back but found herself yanked against the wringer. A sick ripping sound filled Faith's ears. Looking down, she saw a fold of her work apron had gotten caught between the rollers. Tugging against the twisted fabric, she fought the washer. It was no good.

She couldn't get loose! With fierce determination, *der umensch* was reeling her in like a fish on the line.

Not again! Faith's thoughts scrambled inside her mind. She couldn't think clearly. Couldn't digest what was happening. For several horrifying moments, she was transported back in time to her childhood. She was caught. Ensnared! What should she do?

Smack!

A large hand appeared in front of her and struck the release button. The rollers immediately let go of Faith's apron and she stumbled back against a solid chest. Strong arms caught her before she fell. With surprise, she stared up into the most beautiful brown eyes she'd ever seen. Eyes that were all too familiar and crinkled with a mixture of irritation and alarm.

Josiah!

Oh, no! She almost groaned out loud. Of all the people in town, why did it have to be Josiah Brenneman who came to her rescue?

"Faith? Is that you?" He spoke her name in shock, seeming as startled as she was.

At the age of twenty-three, he hadn't changed. Not one bit. Regaining her balance, she stared at his attractive face. The lean cheeks, long nose and full, perfect lips that had always smiled so easily. He still wore the hard black work boots, broadfall pants, suspenders and white shirt of a plain Amish man. But he wasn't plain. Not in any way. Though she hadn't seen him in four long years, she knew him so well. At one time, he'd been the man of her dreams. But not anymore. She'd moved on. They didn't know each other now and she didn't love him anymore. But she had undoubtedly broken his heart when she left town without saying goodbye.

"Josiah, wh-what are you doing here?" she asked.

The back door stood ajar. He must have come in through there. With the clamor of the washing machine, she hadn't heard him step inside.

He frowned. "I could ask you the same thing."

He spoke in *Deitsch*, the language their Amish people used among themselves.

She didn't know what to say. A jagged thatch of dark brown hair fell over his high forehead. Though he needed a haircut, he was more handsome than any man had a right to be, yet he never seemed to know it. After all, vanity wasn't part of their culture. It led to *Hochmut*, the pride of men. Appearances weren't important to them, but she noticed anyway.

"Are you *allrecht*?" he asked, his low voice filled with frustration and concern.

Stepping back, she was desperate to put some distance between them. She turned her face aside, trying to cool her heated cheeks. For the moment, she was free of *der umensch* but now had a greater dilemma to deal with. Since her return, she'd hoped to avoid just three people at all costs. And Josiah was at the top of the list.

"*Ja*, I'm fine. I…I came home because *Aent* Fern died." She spoke as if that was obvious.

"You weren't here for her funeral last week." His voice carried a hint of accusation.

No, and she felt guilty about that. But she couldn't explain why. Not to Josiah. Not to anyone. Hope had died in childbirth three years earlier. If her abusive *Englisch* boyfriend's parents knew they had a three-year-old granddaughter running around town, they might try to take her away. And Faith couldn't allow that to happen, no matter what.

"I came home as soon as I received Bishop Yoder's letter," Faith said.

Josiah's mouth dropped open in shock. "The bishop knew where to find you?"

Her thoughts scattered. "Um, I guess so. I suppose *Aent* Fern gave him my address."

He released a low sigh of impatience. "I still don't understand why you left in the first place."

Of course he didn't. And she could never explain it to him. Not without telling him how Hope had come home late one night, her left wrist broken and her face bruised and bloodied. Brian Clarke, Hope's *Englisch* boyfriend, had beaten her when she'd tried to break up with him. It hadn't been the first time he'd hit her but it'd been the most brutal.

When she saw the state of her niece, Aunt Fern had driven Hope to the local hospital, where a doctor had patched her up. Early the next morning, Aunt Fern packed the two twins' sparse belongings into a battered suitcase and drove them both to the bus station, where she bought them a one-way ticket to Akron, Ohio. There, they had lived with a distant widowed cousin. They had planned to return in a few months, but shortly after they'd arrived in Akron, Hope discovered she was expecting a baby. Faith would have returned to Josiah in Riverton, but she couldn't abandon her twin sister. Not when Hope needed her so much. And when Hope died in childbirth eight months later, Faith then had Adel to look after. The sweetest child on earth, as far as Faith was concerned.

Less than a year after Adel's birth, Aunt Fern wrote

Faith to tell her that Brian had died in a DUI accident. But Brian had a wealthy, domineering *familye* and Faith didn't want to take them on should they decide to fight for custody of Adel.

"I wanted to be here for *Aent* Fern. I really did," Faith said, knowing Josiah wouldn't understand.

"Then, why weren't you?"

Oh, that hurt. More than Faith could say. But she couldn't be two places at once. *Familye* was everything to the Amish. It was everything to Faith. And she hated that Josiah might think she'd neglected her aunt. Until she'd received Bishop Yoder's letter explaining that Fern had died and she was her aunt's only heir, Faith didn't think anyone in this community knew where she was. Without delay, she'd loaded Adel on a bus home. But she didn't plan to stay. As soon as possible, she'd sell the farm and return to Akron, where Adel would be safe.

Glancing at Josiah, Faith didn't answer his question. After all, she owed him no explanation.

"I...I came as soon as I could," she said.

He frowned, then leaned over to pick up his black felt hat. In rushing to her aid, it must have been knocked to the floor. He dusted it off against his thigh, then held it with one strong hand. He wore no beard, which meant he still wasn't married. And for some reason, that made Faith feel terribly sad. Because she wanted him to move on with his life and be happy. He deserved that and so much more.

"*Danke* for rescuing me," she said, releasing a slight laugh.

He glanced at the washer, his forehead crinkled in bewilderment. "Why didn't you just hit the release bar?"

She stared at him and blinked. "I…I don't know why. You know I detest this machine."

Of course he knew. At one time, there hadn't been anything she couldn't confide in him. She wanted to tell him about Hope's baby, too. But she didn't dare. Even if he promised to keep her secret, an innocent slip of the tongue could prove devastating for Adel.

Josiah tilted his head to one side in that quizzical gesture that told her he was annoyed. "The lever is right here."

He pointed at the bar on top of the wringer that said *push to release*. Feeling foolish, Faith's face flooded with heat. All she could think was it'd been four years since she'd used *der umensch*. In Akron, her cousin had washed their clothes and Faith had gladly hung them out to dry, then gathered everything in and folded and put it all away. But in her terror, she'd completely forgotten to push the release bar.

"I…I didn't think about it," she said.

"Mammi! Mammi!"

Whirling around, she stared as Adel raced into the room and flung her little arms around Faith's legs. Dressed in a long, plain blue dress almost identical to Faith's, the tiny girl's feet were bare as she gazed shyly at Josiah with wide, curious eyes. Eyes that looked identical to Hope's. Josiah stared back, his mouth dropping open in startled wonder.

Dead silence filled the room.

"I'm here, Adel. It's *allrecht*. This is Josiah, an old friend of mine. You can say *hallo* to him," Faith said, still speaking in *Deitsch*.

Faith picked up the girl and held her close. She realized if she hadn't left Riverton four years earlier, she would have remained right here and married Josiah. Though he hadn't formally proposed, they'd discussed marriage a couple of times. By now, they might even have a child the age of Adel. Or possibly two children. And thinking about her lost opportunities caused a heavy dose of regret to flood Faith's heart.

"You…you have a *dochder*?" Josiah spoke in a hoarse whisper.

Faith closed her eyes for several seconds, wishing she were anywhere but here. How she hated to hurt this man any more than she'd already done, but it couldn't be helped. When she peered at him again, she could almost see him mentally calculating how old Adel was. The urge to tell him the truth was on the tip of Faith's tongue, but she clenched her teeth and didn't speak the words. She didn't dare. Nothing was more important than keeping Adel safe.

"Adel is mine," she said with finality.

Okay, it wasn't a lie. Adel was hers. On her death-bed, Hope had made Faith promise to keep the baby safe and raise Adel as her own. Then, when the child's birth certificate arrived in the mail several weeks later, Faith discovered her sister had written in Faith's name as the mother and left the father's name blank. Because they were identical twins, Faith realized Hope was try-ing to protect Adel and keep Brian from discovering he had a child. Faith had remained in Akron, longing to return to Josiah in Riverton. While her widowed cousin tended Adel, Faith had helped on the farm and worked part-time as a waitress to pay her bills.

The months had passed, turning into a year, then three. In her weekly letters, Aunt Fern had advised

Faith to remain in Akron until enough time had lapsed that Adel would be safe. Apparently, before he died, Brian had been looking for Hope among the Amish and even came to Aunt Fern's farm to ask where she'd gone. Of course, Aunt Fern had told him nothing. And because she had kept their secret, Brian's *familye* knew nothing about Adel. Worried that news might get back to them, Faith never dared write to tell Josiah where she was. Apparently before her death, Fern had given the bishop Faith's address. The fewer people who knew about Adel and her secret birth, the better.

With her cute button nose, head full of blond curls and sweet disposition, it was easy to adore the child. And since Adel's birth, Faith had raised and loved the tiny girl as her own. The only thing that might give the truth away was Adel's eyes. Faith and Hope were identical twins, but their eyes were different shades of blue. Hope's eyes were a light blue color, much like a robin's egg. Faith's eyes were a dark, cerulean blue that drew people's attention wherever she went. But Adel had inherited her mother's lighter eyes.

Josiah blinked, looking hurt and stunned, as if Faith had just slapped him hard across the face.

"You…you're married?" he asked, his tone incredulous.

Faith's cheeks burned with embarrassment. The implications were clear. Thankfully, she hadn't been baptized at the time of Adel's birth, so she couldn't be shunned for having a child out of wedlock. Faith was innocent of any wrongdoing but she couldn't tell Josiah that. Instead, she lifted her chin an inch higher, prepared to accept his disapproval. He could judge her all he liked. But keeping her sister's child safe was more important than her battered dignity.

"*Ne*, I have never married," Faith said.

Josiah could hardly believe what he was hearing. Four years. That's how long it had been since Faith left town without saying goodbye. They'd had a little spat and he'd said some things he hadn't meant. The next day, he'd gone over to her house to apologize and discovered she was gone. He'd begged her aunt Fern to tell him where she was, so he could go after her. But Fern had refused. She'd told him Faith would return one day soon. For the time being, Faith needed time away. A little vacation.

Four years was not what he would consider a short vacation. Now he could hardly believe Faith was finally home again. He looked away, trying not to stare at her lovely face. She hadn't changed in all this time. She still had the exquisite, rosy complexion, impudent nose, and brilliant blue eyes. Eyes that were once filled with happy, innocent light and a deep, abiding love for him. Now they held a hint of sadness and distrust. And Josiah couldn't help wondering what she'd been doing all this time. Where had she been living and who had she been with? And what had led her to give birth to a child out of wedlock?

By his calculations, Faith must have had Adel within a year after leaving Riverton. If Faith had really loved him, their minor quarrel wouldn't matter. Surely it wasn't important enough to cause her to leave town. Or was it?

Now she had a child. Why would Faith get herself caught with another man's baby so soon after leaving him? Nothing made sense. All he could figure was that she'd never really loved him. And that hurt most of all.

"You've been gone a long time. Why did you *komm* home?" he asked, trying not to sound grouchy and skeptical. After all, it wasn't for him to judge. She could live her life as she chose. But her actions still stung him more than he could say.

Faith lifted a hand, indicated the house and spoke as if the reason was obvious. "My *aent* Fern died, of course. I wanted to pay my respects."

"Are you going to stay this time?" he asked.

She shook her head. "*Ne*, I'm just here to get the place ready for sale. Then, Adel and I will leave again."

Hmm. He never would have believed she was just after her aunt's money. But that's how it appeared. He realized he didn't know her anymore. Perhaps he never had. Hope had always been the worldly twin. Maybe Faith was more like her sister than he knew. And though he'd gotten over this woman a couple of years ago, her words brought a sinking emptiness to his chest.

He looked at the little girl again. Adel. Faith's daughter. A cute, guileless child with big, soft blue eyes. Lovely, just like her mother.

"Hi." The girl's voice was high and sweet. Her timid smile showed an endearing dimple in each cheek.

"You speak English?" he asked in surprise.

Adel tilted her head in confusion and glanced at Faith.

"*Ne*, she speaks *Deitsch*, though she's picked up a few English words along the way," Faith supplied.

So. Had they been living among the *Englisch*? Faith still wore the prayer *kapp*, plain lavender dress, white cape and apron, and black shoes of an Amish woman, although her apron was now shredded by the wringer. She must still be Amish. But where had she been living? He couldn't believe she was really here. With a child of her own.

And no husband.

"Bishop Yoder said the new owner of the place would be arriving this week, but I didn't know it was you. I thought your *aent* would leave the place to one of her nephews." He couldn't think of anything better to say.

Faith shifted her weight nervously, holding Adel against her hip. "*Ne*, she left the place to me. All my cousins already have farms of their own. Remember Hope and I are quite a bit younger than them and we were orphaned."

Adel leaned against her mother's throat and peered at him with big, shy eyes that he thought were more the lighter shade of Hope's eyes. But since Faith and Hope had been identical twins, he didn't question the subtle difference.

He nodded. "*Ja*, that must be it. I guess since your sister is gone and Fern raised you, it's logical that she left the place to you."

Faith flinched, as if the reminder was painful to her.

"You knew about Hope?" she asked.

He inclined his head. "*Ja*, Fern told me she'd died a few years ago. I was sorry to hear of her passing. I know you two were close. I thought…I thought with her gone, you might *komm* home. But you didn't."

Faith looked away, as if she didn't want to talk about it. Okay, he could take a hint. But he couldn't stop the unanswered questions from roiling around inside his head. He just had to ask one more question…

"Why did you leave like that, Faith? You didn't even speak to me first. It never made sense. And then, you show up here with a *kind* of your own. I still don't understand," he said.

Okay, now he'd done it. Maybe he shouldn't have said all that. He hated exposing his broken heart to her. Hated for her to know how much she'd hurt him when she left.

"I'm sorry, Josiah. There wasn't time to talk to you. I had to leave immediately. I couldn't return until now. That's all I can tell you," she said.

"Then, you didn't leave because of our little argument?" he asked.

She blinked in bewilderment. "What argument?"

Had she forgotten, or was she pretending?

"Remember, I told you I wanted ten *kinder*," he said. "You insisted you wanted no more than six. You didn't leave because of that?"

She snorted. "*Ne*, that isn't the reason I left."

He shook his head, feeling more perplexed than ever. If she hadn't abandoned him because of their disagreement, then why did she go?

"I really don't want to talk about it any more. It was a long time ago. Let's leave it in the past. I…I hope you can understand," she said, her eyes glazing over with sadness and a bit of defense.

"*Ne*, I don't, but I guess you have your reasons," he said.

"I'm sorry, Josiah. Please forgive me. I never meant to hurt you. But…the situation wasn't something I could control. You see…Hope needed me," she said.

Hope! With her worldly ways, the girl was constantly getting into trouble. And Faith was always bailing her out. Stealing watermelons from Zeke Burkholder's field. Breaking Deacon Albrecht's shop window with a baseball. Slipping out of the house late at night to attend the high school prom with her *Englisch* boyfriend. Cutting her hair and wearing makeup. But now Hope was dead, and Faith was the one with an illegitimate child. Sadly, Josiah feared Hope's wild ways had rubbed off on Faith.

He stared at her, wishing she'd explain. Longing for some logical reason for her sudden departure. No, he didn't understand. But right now, Faith looked nervous and wary and he sensed there was something she wasn't telling him. Something big. And he realized this wasn't the time to press her for answers.

He shrugged it off and turned toward the washing machine. "*Ach*, it doesn't matter. I moved on years ago. What's done is done."

He stepped over to the window, desperate to put some distance between them. But deep inside, his heart ached. The Lord taught that he should turn the other cheek. Anger was not of *Gott*. And yet, that's how Josiah felt inside. Good and mad. And filled with doubts. For four long years, he'd been assisting Fern Miller with her farm. The woman had been in her late eighties. With Faith and Hope gone, Fern had needed lots of help. He hadn't known what was in her will when she died three weeks earlier but he'd known her heir would soon come to claim the farm. He thought it would be a man…one of Faith's male cousins from back east. At Fern's funeral, Bishop Yoder had asked Josiah to assist the new owner as much as possible. And because he'd loved Fern, Josiah had agreed. But when he'd arrived today, never in his wildest dreams had he expected to find Faith Mast standing here. The woman he'd once loved more than anything else in the world. She'd broken his heart. A woman he could neither forgive nor forget.

"So, you're going to sell the place?" he asked.

Preoccupied with a ribbon on Faith's prayer *kapp*, Adel was humming a nonsensical tune to herself, her voice low and pleasant. Though Faith's golden hair was tucked beneath her prayer *kapp*, a long strand had escaped to caress her soft cheek. He yearned to reach up and tuck it back into place but resisted the urge. After all, they'd grown apart and no longer loved each other. She'd chosen her path and must now walk it alone, without him.

He looked away.

"*Ja*, as soon as I get things in order," she said.

"It's fallen into disrepair, but it's still a *gut* farm," he said.

Good enough to buy himself. In addition to Cherry Creek meandering through the middle of the property, it included five acres of apple orchards, twenty acres of barley, twenty for pastureland, fifty for hay and five acres of forestland. On top of that, it had a sturdy white frame house with indoor plumbing. The outbuildings included a large, solid barn, sheds and corrals. With Fern's husband having been gone six years, a lot of things had been neglected. But it wouldn't take much to remedy that. Depending on Faith's asking price, Josiah wondered if he could afford to make the purchase himself. Currently, he still lived at home with his parents. He was the eighth of nine children. All but his youngest brother had married and moved on, with places of their own. But after Faith broke up with him, Josiah had no reason to purchase a farm for himself. Instead, he'd stayed put, working for his father and saving almost every penny he earned. Wondering if the hollow feeling in his heart would ever cease.

"The place is definitely worn down. It needs a lot of work," Faith said.

So, she'd noticed.

"*Ja*, your *aent* Fern insisted I let the barley fields go fallow. They've all gone to weed now. But I've been cutting her hay each year and watering the pastures and orchards so they wouldn't die. I hired some Amish men to help me pick her apples, so she'd have an income to live on. She wouldn't let me do any more than that, no matter how hard I tried. I offered to work for free, but she refused."

"That sounds like *Aent* Fern. She wouldn't want to accept charity," she said.

"It was no bother. Except for her old road horse, she even let all her livestock go."

Faith glanced toward the window. "But I see twenty head of cattle grazing in the south pasture."

He nodded. "Those are mine. I've been renting the field from your *aent*. She doesn't own any farm animals now. Not even chickens. The work just became too much for her, but I did what I could. I…I was the one who found her when she died."

"Oh." Faith's lips curved in a circle. She looked away but not before he caught a hint of pain and remorse in her lovely blue eyes.

For the umpteenth time, he couldn't help wondering why she'd abandoned her aunt. What had induced her to live somewhere else and have a child out of wedlock? Unlike Hope, not once had Faith expressed a desire to leave their Amish faith. While Hope had chased after an *Englisch* boyfriend, Faith had always been so devout. So good, diligent and predictable.

"I…I was wondering if you might stay on and help me do some repairs and work. Just until I can get the house and farm ready to sell," she said.

He hesitated.

She hurried on, as if she feared he might refuse. "I'll pay you, of course. I have the money *Aent* Fern left me."

Oh, how badly he wanted to decline. But vengeance wasn't in his nature. *Gott* wouldn't approve of him holding a grudge. No matter how much Josiah wanted to say no, he just couldn't do it. He'd never been able to deny Faith anything. Not since they were young children, growing up together in this valley.

"I will help you, starting tomorrow morning, after my chores are finished at home. But right now, I've got to check the cattle, then pick up some groceries at the store in town for my *mudder*," he said.

He was going to regret this. He just knew it.

Faith released a whoosh of air, as if she'd been holding her breath. "That sounds fine. I'll see you tomorrow, then."

Turning, he walked out the back door, closing it quietly behind him. As he headed toward the barn, he thought he shouldn't have said so much. He shouldn't have let her know how badly she'd injured him by disappearing four years earlier. But maybe she needed to know how her careless actions had hurt him. No matter what, they could never be a couple again. From her responses, he could see she didn't love him anymore. Well, that suited him fine. He would work for her until the farm was ready to sell. He might even be able to scrape together the funds to buy the place for himself. But that was it. Because he didn't love her anymore, either. And he sure wouldn't trust her. No, sirree. Never again. Especially not with his heart.

Chapter Two

Kneeling on the front porch, Faith scraped another area of peeling paint off the side of the house. With her back to the main yard, she kept her ears tuned to the happy sounds of Adel playing on the dried grass behind her. To see if she could bring back the yellowed lawn, Faith had hooked up the garden hose and turned on the sprinkler. The flower beds were filled with weeds and dried leaves. Faith needed to rake them out but they weren't a priority now. The early spring weather was perfect for planting barley and hay but she wasn't sure she wanted to commit to the crops if she wouldn't be here for the harvest. Maybe she'd seek Josiah's advice when he finally arrived later that morning.

Glancing over her shoulder, she peered at Adel, who was standing just at the edge of the sprinkler. She held her little hand out to catch the spray of water, yet she wasn't near enough to get soaked.

"Don't get too close, my little dilly bean," Faith said with a laugh.

"I'n not," Adel called back in her tiny voice. Then her forehead furrowed in question. "Why not?"

Faith turned back to her chore, chipping away at the cracked paint. "Because you'll get wet and then you'll get cold. It's a nice day but there's still a nip of frost in the air."

Adel tilted her head in question. "Nip?"

"*Ja*, it means just a little bit of cold," Faith said, more than used to the girl's quizzical nature.

She'd learned this child was really smart. Mothering Adel required patience and answering lots of questions.

"Ohh." Adel nodded, as if she understood completely.

Finished with the area on one side of the front door, Faith stood and arched her lower back to ease the ache. As she studied her work with a critical eye, she realized this was going to be a huge job and take a long time. Maybe she should dip into the savings account her aunt had left her and hire it out. A professional painter could come from Cañon City, fifteen miles away, and have it finished in no time. The sooner she got the work done, the sooner she could list the farm and leave town. Although *Aent* Fern had left her a tidy savings account, she was loath to spend anything that wasn't necessary until she was certain she could buy her own home in Akron. Resigned to doing the chore herself, she knelt on the porch and started scraping another area.

"*Guder mariye.*" A cheerful greeting came from behind her.

Faith glanced over her shoulder and saw Josiah carrying a bucket and tall ladder, which he leaned against the upper level of the house. He'd tucked several paint rags into the waistband of his plain broadfall pants. Apparently he planned to help with this chore.

"Hallo," she returned, lurching to her feet. "I...I didn't know you'd arrived."

"I came in about ten minutes ago. You were in the house and probably didn't hear me."

"Oh," she said, thinking how silly she must sound.

He jutted his chin toward the farmhouse. "Looks like you're getting ready to paint."

"*Ja*, inside and out. But the job is proving to be more than I planned on. I'm afraid it hasn't been done in years and it needs painting badly if I'm to sell the place," she said.

"Don't worry. The work will go along quick enough now that I'm here. Many hands make light work," he said, his voice sounding cheerful.

Aunt Fern had said the same thing many times and it brought a nostalgic stab of sadness to Faith's heart. As Josiah came to stand beside her, she wished she could share his outlook. He'd always been so confident and in control. So positive and self-assured. No task was ever too much for him. He tackled everything in life with cheer and optimism.

"But shouldn't you be tending to the farm?" she asked.

"I've been meaning to ask you about that. The orchard and pastures are in *gut* shape and I've already planted the spring hay. But do you want to grow barley, too?"

She glanced toward the weedy field, wondering what her uncle Noah would say if he saw how derelict it had become. "I definitely want it plowed, to turn the weeds under. And the garden spot needs cultivation, too. But I'm not sure about growing a crop this year. Do you think the farm would show better and sell more quickly if we planted the barley and vegetable garden?"

He nodded. "Most certainly. Even if you give the produce away, it's a shame to leave fertile ground fallow. I'll tell you what. Let's take the rest of the week to get the outside of the house painted. Then, the following Monday, I'll focus on plowing and planting the barley. I'll mulch your garden too, but I'll let you plant the vegetables. If nothing else, it'll keep you busy while you're here, and when you sell the place, the harvest won't be your concern."

She glanced at him, a sad feeling settling inside her chest. The thought of not being here for the reaping upset her more than she realized. Short of leaving Josiah, leaving the place would be one of the hardest things she'd ever done. Selling the farm was like losing another beloved friend. Over the past four years, she'd looked forward to nothing more than coming home to stay. She'd always thought Aunt Fern would be here and realized how much she'd taken her aunt and uncle for granted. Still, Faith would feel better seeing her home spiffed up before she had to leave. And after that, her memories would have to sustain her. But nothing took precedence over Adel. The child was innocent of what had happened in the past. Not even Faith's own dreams of a happy marriage and *familye* could take priority over the little girl.

"*Allrecht.* Let's do it," Faith said.

Josiah smiled, his dark eyes sparkling with approval. Then he frowned and stepped aside, as if he'd suddenly remembered who she was and that she'd abandoned him without a backward glance.

Once again, she thought about telling him the truth. But she feared if she did, it'd be the second greatest mistake of her life.

"*Hallo*, Ziah."

Faith turned as Adel clutched her hand with her tiny fingers. The child was gazing up at the man with a timid smile.

Josiah's face lit up. Faith realized with a modicum of relief that he held no grudge against her little girl.

"*Ach, hallo*, little dilly bean. That is what your *mammi* called you, ain't so?" he asked with a teasing grin.

Adel scowled, pretending to be insulted. "I'n no dilly bean. I'n Del."

Unable to say her own name properly, the girl drilled a finger against her chest for emphasis.

"*Ach*, then you don't like being called dilly bean?" he asked, faking a surprised expression.

Adel looked down, playing coy as she scuffed the point of her black shoe against a rock. "Sometimes I do."

He laughed and so did Faith. She couldn't help it. This little girl had brought her so much joy over the past three years. The child had made Faith's time away from home more bearable.

Josiah bent down on his haunches in front of the girl but he didn't touch her. "Dilly bean is a most unusual name. Tell me, how did you come by it?"

Adel looked up at Faith, her eyes filled with uncertainty. It was obvious she didn't know.

"*Ach*, when Adel was no more than a year old, my cousin was bottling dilly beans and Adel insisted on eating one. With all that sour vinegar, I thought Adel would spit it out, but she ate every bit and asked for more. And ever since that time, she's loved them. So, I started calling her my little dilly bean and the name has kind of stuck."

Josiah came to his feet and Faith felt dwarfed by his height. "Your cousin? Which one?"

Faith clamped her mouth shut, realizing her error. She'd just revealed a crucial part of her past to him that could prove fatal. And all she could hope was that he didn't remember she had a distant widowed cousin living in Akron, Ohio.

When she didn't speak, he hurried on without missing a beat as he looked at Adel again.

"*Ach*, it's okay to eat dilly beans as long as you don't act like one. You don't want to have a sour disposition," he said.

Adel crinkled her eyes in confusion. "*Mammi*, what's dip-sis-hion?" She stumbled over the long word. Like Josiah's name, she couldn't quite manage to say the entire thing correctly.

"A disposition is how you act. A sweet disposition is someone who acts nice. A sour disposition is someone who acts grouchy and rude. But I don't think you have that problem. You're mostly kind and even-tempered," she said, pressing the girl against her leg for a quick hug.

Adel smiled with delight. "*Ach*, I'n a sweet dilly bean."

Faith blinked and stared at the girl. How had she grasped the concept of sweet and sour so quickly? Faith had always known Adel was clever, but sometimes she thought the child was exceptionally bright. And that brought Faith a motherly pride she couldn't deny. But since pride was of the world, she kept it to herself.

"And I'd best get to work. This house isn't going to paint itself," Josiah said.

While Faith moved the sprinkler to another spot,

he reached for another scraper she'd laid beside her work tools.

"Ziah, I help?" Adel asked.

"Sure, dilly bean. Hand me those paintbrushes. I'll put them over here on the table so they'll stay clean until we're ready to use them." He held out a hand and waited patiently while Adel scrambled to do his bidding.

Watching the man and little girl together, Faith couldn't help thinking Adel had fallen for his charisma, just like Faith had done years earlier. But knowing they were leaving soon, Faith was determined to resist Josiah's charms this second time around. It had required everything in her to leave him. Then it had taken several years to stop loving him. If she wasn't careful, she'd end up with another broken heart when she took Adel and left town again.

In an effort to avoid Faith as much as possible, Josiah moved the tall ladder over to the south side of the house. Ensuring he didn't damage the juniper bushes below, he set the bottom rung on the edge of the dried lawn. Taking a scraper in hand, he climbed up to the second story. With short, even strokes, he scraped the peeling paint away from the wood siding. For over an hour, he worked, pondering the questions that had troubled him for several years. Discovering that Adel had been given the nickname of "dilly bean" after eating Faith's cousin's pickled beans led him to believe they'd been living in Ohio. Josiah knew Faith had a lot of relatives in Millersburg. It was the logical place she would have gone. But he still couldn't understand why she'd left in the first place or why she was so evasive about it now.

Having finished an area of scraping, he stepped down off the ladder, moved it over to another position and climbed up again. Midway up, he wasn't focused on his work and lost his footing. Before he knew what was happening, he felt the ladder tip. He clawed madly for the side of the house to stabilize himself but his fingernails grazed the wooden structure. In a scant moment, he prepared himself to see stars. He felt himself falling and a cry tore from his throat. The ground slammed up to meet him. Pain ripped through his body and the air was knocked from his lungs. He lay among the thick juniper bushes, stunned, hurting and gasping for breath. Thankfully, he hadn't hit his head.

"*Mammi! Mammi!* Ziah fall down."

Little Adel stood over him, peering at his face with concern. Then she raced around to the front of the house, only to return moments later with Faith hot on her heels.

"Josiah! Are you *allrecht*?"

Faith knelt beside him, pressing her hands against his chest and shoulders, as if checking for broken bones.

"I…I'm okay," he said, trying to sit up.

He fought to take an inhale, struggling to fill his lungs with air.

Faith helped him, her touch gentle as she extricated him from the juniper bushes. Gradually, he became aware of a sharp pain in his right knee and elbow, and a long tear in his shirt where a deep scratch marred his abdomen. He must have struck the side of the house when he fell.

"Can you sit up?" Faith asked.

He nodded. "I think so."

Letting her help him, he sat for several moments, catching his breath and flexing his ankles and wrists to determine if they were broken. He was vaguely aware of Adel hovering nearby, her small hand resting against his shoulder in a consoling gesture.

"Ziah fall down," she said, her voice filled with sympathy and her face torn by worry.

Reaching up, he patted the child's hand. "Don't worry, dilly bean. I'm okay."

She smiled and he realized she was a compassionate child, a character trait he thought she must have learned from her *mamm*.

"Can you stand?" Faith asked.

He nodded. "I don't think I have any broken bones."

Faith nodded and plucked needlelike leaves from off his clothes and hair. "Thank goodness for the junipers. I think they broke your fall."

He gave a shallow laugh. "*Ja*, you're right."

Holding on to her, he slowly tested his weight as he stood. His knee was definitely sore but he determined it wasn't anything that wouldn't heal.

"*Ne*, nothing is broken," he said.

"But you're bleeding," Faith observed, stepping away to give him some space.

Looking down, he saw a long scratch on his side had soaked a small area of his torn shirt with blood.

"*Komm* into the house. I'll clean and bandage the wound for you," Faith offered.

He glanced at the position of the sun in the sky. Since there were several hours of work remaining in the day, he agreed. Otherwise, he'd just go home and let his mother tend to him. But he couldn't lose a day of work because he'd taken a tumble. There was too much to be done.

Faith clasped his arm and accompanied him up the front steps. He moved stiffly, feeling as though he'd been bludgeoned by a baseball bat. By the time he sat on a wooden chair in the kitchen, he was moving more easily.

"I'll be right back." Faith left him there with Adel.

The child's soft blue eyes crinkled with empathy as she peered at him. "Ziah hurt?"

He showed what he hoped was a reassuring smile. "*Ne*, not bad. I'll be fine. Don't worry, dilly. I just need a bandage and I'll be right back to work."

Faith returned at that moment with some antiseptic, scissors, gauze and medical tape. She knelt beside him and he held up his tattered shirt while she administered to him. Her touch was infinitely gentle and he couldn't deny the warmth of her fingertips against his skin as she dabbed the nasty scrape with disinfectant. After cutting pieces of gauze, she taped them over the wound. Then she looked up into his eyes. For several profound moments, he felt lost. Her lips parted in a quiet sigh. And that's when he knew. Although they were no longer in love, the physical attraction they'd once shared was still there, just as if it had never left. From her startled expression, she felt it, too.

She stood abruptly and backed away. She busied herself with tidying the medical supplies and tossing the used cotton balls into a garbage can.

"*Ach*, I'd best get back to work. Maybe you should go *heemet* and put your feet up for the rest of the day," she said, her back turned to him.

"*Ne*, I'm fine. We can't afford to miss any time if we're to get your fields plowed and planted. I know you're eager to accomplish a number of tasks so you can sell the place," he said.

His unintentional reminder was like dousing them both with ice water. Once the farm was ready for selling, she would leave the area for good and never return.

Bracing a hand against the table, he stood and adjusted his torn shirt before tucking it into the top of his pants. He arranged his suspenders, noticing one of the clips was broken.

She faced him, gesturing at the tear. "If you'll bring your shirt back tomorrow, I'll do my best to wash out the blood. I can mend it, and your suspenders, too."

Her offer felt too personal and domestic to him, an everyday task a wife would do for her husband. And for that reason alone, he declined.

"That won't be necessary. My *mamm* will take care of it for me."

Stepping over to the door, he patted Adel's soft cheek as he opened the screen and, without a word, strode outside. Paying more attention to his chore, he repositioned the ladder and tested it for security. Then, with scraper in hand, he slowly climbed up and resumed his task of removing old, peeling paint from the side of the house. Minutes later, he heard the front screen door open and clap closed and then Faith's voice as she spoke to Adel in the front yard. No doubt Faith would continue her work on the porch, too. They didn't speak again, and when evening came, he heard the woman and child go back inside the house to prepare their supper.

Putting his tools away, Josiah went to the barn, harnessed his road horse to his buggy and pulled out of the yard without bidding Faith farewell. As he passed the house, he saw her standing at the kitchen window, which he knew sat above the sink. Lifting a hand, he waved. She did likewise, but he caught a look of reticence on her face and wondered if she disliked him now. Or did she simply feel guilty for having a child out of wedlock? He wasn't sure what she thought.

When she'd tended his wound, a cascade of old feelings had wafted over him. But he knew it was a farce. What they'd shared once had meant nothing. Not a lasting love that could endure the test of time. It was better for him to focus his attention on one of the other young women in his congregation. Trina Graber was interested in him. Though he was six years her senior, he knew she'd marry him if he proposed. But somehow, she just didn't stack up to what he was after in a wife. He told himself it was because she was so young. She needed time to mature. Maybe he should take another look. He had to marry someone. He'd already suffered one broken heart and was determined never to fall for Faith again. No, sirree. Not in a trillion years.

Chapter Three

The very next day, Faith wasn't surprised when Bishop Yoder's buggy pulled into the front yard. In fact, she was shocked he hadn't shown up sooner. No doubt he was busy planting his own crops. Or perhaps it had taken time for news of her return to get around. Knowing the Amish gossip mill, she figured the entire *Gmay*, her Amish community there in Riverton, knew she was back in town. Surely Josiah had told his parents and word had spread from there.

Wiping her damp hands on a dish towel, she peeked into the living room, where Adel was playing quietly with Martha, a faceless rag doll Faith had made for her several months earlier. The soft toy figure wore a tiny version of Amish dress with bright red hair made of yarn.

Kneeling beside the sofa, Adel posed Martha's arms, as if they were saying evening prayers. Then the child laid the doll against a pillow and covered it with a blanket as she hummed a quiet lullaby.

Waves of emotion washed over Faith, feelings of love so strong that she almost cried. This was the exact bedtime routine she went through each night with Adel and it warmed Faith's heart to know her little girl was learning by her example.

"Adel, I'm going outside for a minute. I'll be back soon," she said.

The girl's head jerked up and she pressed a single finger to her lips as she whispered to her, "Shh, *Mammi*. Martha sleeping."

Faith's mouth twitched and she forced herself not to smile. But it didn't matter. Adel had already turned her attention back to Martha and didn't notice Faith was struggling not to laugh at this precious, endearing moment.

A knock sounded on the back door and Faith hurried to the kitchen to answer it. Tossing the dish towel aside, she opened the screen door.

"Bishop Yoder! How nice to see you," she said, speaking casually as she greeted the man.

Because she didn't want Adel to overhear their conversation, she stepped out onto the deck with him.

"Do you mind if we talk out here?" She pointed at a set of four Adirondack chairs her great-uncle Noah had made years earlier. They were still quite solid but, like everything else on this farm, they needed sanding and a fresh coat of paint.

"*Ja*, that would be best. Is Adel inside?" he asked, stepping over to one of the chairs.

So. He knew about her little girl, too. Word had definitely traveled fast.

"*Ja*, she's playing with her *bopp*. We can have a few minutes without interruption."

Faith perched on the edge of her seat across from the bishop. She dreaded this chat. What if he criticized her for having a child out of wedlock? She could even be shunned. And knowing in her heart that she was innocent of wrongdoing, that would be the hardest thing to bear. But she'd do it…for Adel.

To make matters worse, Josiah stood in the driveway near the bishop's horse and buggy. Whatever the bishop said to her, she didn't want Josiah to overhear. For the Amish, one of the greatest deterrents to avoid sin was that their lives and business were an open book. Everyone soon found out what they were doing. And Faith couldn't allow word to spread that Adel was really Hope's daughter. So, whatever the bishop had to say, Faith would face it with prayer and courage.

With a quick glance in their direction, Josiah led the horse to the watering trough. While the animal drank, he stood patiently, easily able to overhear her conversation if she spoke too loudly.

Taking a deep breath, Faith met the bishop's steady gaze.

"Um, what brings you out my way?" she asked softly.

"I just wanted to see how you're getting on." The bishop's voice sounded friendly enough. He watched Josiah for several moments, his gray eyes filled with quiet thoughtfulness. "Josiah is a conscientious young man and a hard worker. I understand he is doing chores for you, to get your farm ready to sell."

She nodded, still speaking low. "*Ja*, he's been a great help already."

The bishop leaned back in his chair and settled his steely gaze on her. That act alone unnerved Faith. More than anything, she hated to have this man's disapproval. He'd always been a kind, considerate leader of their *Gmay*. But that was back when she was young and hadn't appeared to violate the tenets of their faith. She didn't want to get crosswise with him.

"I'm sorry you weren't here for Fern's funeral," he said. "We held off her burial as long as we could. I suppose you finally received my letter?"

"*Ja*, but I'm afraid it arrived late. Our mailman gave it to our neighbor down the road and it sat on her kitchen counter until she finally remembered to walk it over to my house. I didn't receive it until two days before I arrived here in town," she said.

"*Ach*, that explains your tardy appearance. I wondered why you didn't *komm* sooner." He dipped his head in understanding.

"*Danke* for letting me know *Aent* Fern had passed away. I...I came as soon as I could," she said, feeling empty and sad because she hadn't been able to say goodbye.

"Maybe you could visit her gravesite to pay your last respects," he suggested.

"*Ja*, I plan to do that. In fact, I was hoping to go later this afternoon."

"*Gut*. She loved you very much, you know."

"I loved her, too," she said.

The bishop showed a soft smile. "She knew that. And she knew you would have been here, if you could."

Faith shifted nervously as she spoke in a soft whisper. "How...how did you know where to find me?"

"Fern told me. Several months before her death, she knew she was ailing. In case she died, she wanted someone she could trust to know what had happened to you and Hope, in case you needed my help," he said.

Taking a quiet inhale, Faith let it go. Her hands trembled and her body was filled with trepidation. Just how much did the bishop really know?

Faith tossed a glance toward Josiah, wishing he would finish watering the horse and leave.

"What…what else did she tell you?" she asked.

The bishop smiled gently and held out a hand, speaking low. "Faith, don't be afraid. Your secret is safe with me. But Fern told me everything. I know Adel is Hope's child and that you're trying to prevent her *Englisch* grandparents from taking her away. I am in full support of her remaining Amish, too."

Faith pressed one hand to her lips as tears blurred her eyes. She peered at Josiah, hoping he hadn't overheard.

"Then you understand why no one must know?" She couldn't keep a note of desperation from filling her shaking voice.

Bishop Yoder nodded. "*Ja*, I understand and agree that it's best to keep knowledge of what happened from getting out. That's why I have told no one. Not even my wife."

She released a slow exhale, realizing she'd been holding her breath.

A rustling sound drew her attention and she looked up as Josiah led the bishop's horse over to stand beneath the shade of a tall elm tree. Had he overheard any part of her conversation? Oh, she hoped not.

When Josiah sauntered over to the barn and disappeared inside, she breathed more easily.

The bishop leaned forward, his gaze pinned on her. "You know, it was Fern's greatest wish that you and Adel would return here where you belong. That's why she left her entire estate to you. So you would *komm* home and stay. Since I wrote to tell you of her passing, I've waited anxiously for your return, so I also could invite you to stay."

A feeling of panic clawed her throat. "But I can't remain here, Bishop. What if Brian's parents find out the truth? They're *Englisch* and have a lot of wealth and influence in our community. They could persuade a judge to take Adel from me. It's best if I get the farm ready to sell and leave as soon as possible."

He frowned and looked toward the corrals, as if considering her words. "You can leave if you choose but I hope you'll stay. Don't become discouraged. I'm confident everything will work out as it should. Remember to have faith. Trust in *Gott*."

Faith was her name and the foundation of her beliefs. But even with Josiah here every day, she felt all alone in the world. Sometimes, she even feared *Gott* had abandoned her. She was nothing but a simple Amish woman. If Brian's parents found out about Adel and sued for custody, what *Englisch* judge would listen to her?

The bishop flashed an understanding smile. "I'm pleased by the sacrifices you've made on Adel's behalf. That alone speaks highly of your character. Your little *maedel* needs a *gut* role model such as you in her life. She is innocent of any wrongdoing, as are you. I'm sure the *gut* Lord will bless you for your efforts. And regardless of whether you remain here or return to Ohio, I will support you in your decision."

She released a sigh of relief, feeling better. Though she was worried about her situation, it felt good to have at least one ally. That wouldn't help her in a court of law but it was better than nothing.

At that moment, Josiah came out of the barn again and Faith jerked nervously in response.

The bishop came to his feet, signaling their interview was over. "As I've said, if there's anything you need, just ask. I've told Josiah to look after you and Adel. I'm leaving you in capable hands."

As Faith stood, she understood his meaning only too well. Being "told" to do something by the bishop was more like an order, except the bishop usually did it so politely. But when Bishop Yoder spoke, the Amish in this community listened. He had a penchant for kindness and doing what was best for his congregation. He always put others first and not once had she ever heard him raise his voice. That's why her people had elected him as their bishop. But he could lay down the law, too. Like the rumbling of thunder off in the distance, one calm word from this man could shake you to the core. At his say-so, the entire *Gmay* would turn their back on Faith, which would make it difficult for her to sell the farm. She would hate to have him as an enemy.

He stepped down off the deck and looked back at her. Josiah joined them, making Faith feel tense and worried. What if he'd overheard even a part of her conversation with the bishop? He could go home and tell his parents, and then it'd spread from there.

"I know you may choose to sell your farm and leave, but now that you're here, I hope you'll stay with us at least a little while." The bishop flashed a wide smile. "And church will be held tomorrow at my farm. I'll look forward to seeing you and Adel there."

Oh, dear. Faith knew what that meant. She'd better show up or he'd be back on her doorstep Monday morning. But she couldn't begrudge this good man.

By inviting her to church, he was only doing his duty in directing her to follow their Savior, Jesus Christ.

"Josiah, I'll leave this farm and its occupants to your proficient care. Faith and Adel plan to pay their respects to Fern's grave later this afternoon. I'd take it as a personal favor if you'd drive them there," the bishop said.

Josiah acquiesced obediently. "Of course I will."

"Gut! Vaarwel." With a nod of farewell, the bishop sauntered over to his horse and buggy.

Faith stood frozen in place. She couldn't move. Couldn't breathe. Whether she liked it or not, Josiah had been assigned to look after her and her farm…and drive her to the cemetery, too.

As she watched Bishop Yoder climb into his buggy and pull out of her driveway, she longed to tell Josiah to go away. She didn't need him to drive her to the cemetery. She could do that herself. She had Aunt Fern's money now and could hire workmen to come in and spruce up the farm, too. She never should have hired Josiah. She didn't need anybody's help.

Or did she?

Though the bishop had told her everything would work out fine, Faith had misgivings. Over the past few years, so many bad things had happened to her and the people she cared about that she'd become overly pessimistic. To add to that load, she now had a lot of hard, manual labor facing her just to get the farm in order so she could sell the place. Whether she liked it or not, she did need Josiah's help and it did her no good to deny it.

A feeling of gloom overshadowed her and she felt almost overwhelmed by it all.

"Is everything okay?" Josiah asked quietly as he stood beside her.

She looked up at him, feeling confused by a rush of emotions. On the one side, she wanted to do this on her own. But on the other, she felt the sudden urge to lean against his solid strength and tell him everything, just so she could hand off the burden to his capable hands. But she couldn't do that, either. Not now, not ever. Not if she wanted to protect Adel.

"*Mammi!* I'n hungry."

Faith whirled around and found the little girl standing behind her. Martha dangled from one of Adel's hands. Though the screen door usually squeaked loudly when it was opened, Faith hadn't heard Adel step outside.

Ignoring Josiah's question, Faith reached to pick up her child and kiss her cheek. "*Ach*, then we'd best get you some breakfast, hadn't we? Then, I've got painting to do."

As she pulled open the screen door, Faith glanced back at Josiah. She hated to ask but good manners dictated that she must. "Have you eaten yet?"

He nodded. "*Ja*, my *mudder* made breakfast early this morning."

"Okay, then." She wished he'd trundle off to the barn.

Taking her cue, he stepped off the deck, then paused to look back at her. "I've already fed Billy. I'll get started on the painting. After lunch, I'll bring the buggy around to take you and Adel to the cemetery."

Faith hesitated. "That would be fine."

"Bye, Ziah." Adel waved one little hand, still clutching Martha to her chest.

"Bye, dilly bean. See you later." He smiled and headed toward the shed.

It was on the tip of Faith's tongue to call him back.

To tell him she could drive herself to the cemetery. But she didn't dare.

What had possessed the bishop to make such a request? Faith had heard that he frequently involved himself in matchmaking among their Amish congregation. Was that what this was about? If so, he could forget it. Because she was not staying. She and Josiah weren't a couple anymore. No matter what the bishop said, she was selling this farm. And that was that.

Pulling the door open wide, Josiah stepped inside the dim interior of the shed and gazed at the row of paint cans lining one wall. Drop cloths, brushes and stirring sticks were stacked in neat piles on a shelf beside the door. Everything in its place. If nothing else, Faith was tidy and hardworking.

They'd finished scraping the house and started painting yesterday. If they worked hard, they could complete the job today. Then, he could turn his attention to plowing the barley fields first thing next week.

Reaching for a bucket and roller, he fought off a feeling of confusion. For several months, Bishop Yoder had known how to contact Faith. Josiah hadn't tried to eavesdrop on their conversation but he'd overheard that much. Years earlier, Josiah had made it clear to everyone in their *Gmay* that he wanted to locate Faith. So, why hadn't the bishop told him where she was? Why had he kept it a secret? None of this made sense.

Making several trips back and forth to the house, Josiah carried the ladder and paint supplies over and set them down. After spreading the drop cloth over Faith's weedy flower bed, he leaned the ladder against the side of the wall. He'd already taped up the windows. Using a flathead screwdriver to pop the lid off a can of paint, he inserted a stick and stirred the viscous stuff to ensure it was blended. Then he poured a liberal amount into a rolling pan. With that and a roller in tow, he climbed the ladder carefully and went to work.

Within twenty minutes, Faith came outside with Adel. After settling the child on a blanket nearby so she could keep an eye on her, Faith got her own roller and moved in tandem nearby. They didn't speak but kept up a steady stream of work, finishing all but the back portion of the house.

"*Mammi*, I have to go," Adel called.

Looking down, Josiah saw the girl was doing an anxious two-step, which spurred Faith into action.

Hiding a smile, he felt a softening inside his chest that seemed rather alien to him. He wondered how Adel had wormed her way into his heart so quickly. Faith was a doting mother and he couldn't help admiring the way she cared for her child and home.

When the girls didn't return immediately, Josiah glanced at the cloudless sky. Lunchtime. No doubt Faith was inside feeding her daughter.

Stepping off the ladder, Josiah sealed the cans of paint and wrapped plastic garbage bags around the rollers and brushes so they wouldn't dry out. Then he hastened to the barn where he retrieved the simple lunch he'd prepared for himself early that morning and consumed it in haste. Within minutes, he had Billy harnessed to the buggy and pulled it up out front of the back door. He didn't have long to wait before Faith and Adel came outside. The child carried a rag doll dressed in a little Amish dress.

"Ziah!" Adel cried when she saw him.

"You ready to go, dilly?" he asked.

"Ja!" She nodded and smiled wide as he lifted her into her safety seat.

He offered his arm to Faith. She hesitated just a moment, then accepted as she climbed into the buggy. Her fingers felt soft and warm against his skin.

"Danke," she said.

"Gaern gscheh," he returned.

Within moments, they were on their way, with Adel sitting between them.

"There's no need to fuss. You don't need to drive us to the cemetery," Faith said.

Josiah paused several moments, thinking this over. *"Ach*, the bishop asked me to do it. He probably wants to make sure you're safe."

Her lips tightened. "Why wouldn't we be? I'm perfectly capable of looking after myself."

"I know," he said. "No one has questioned your capabilities, Faith. But I'd feel terrible if something happened to you and Adel when I could do something to prevent it. I'm sure the bishop feels the same way."

Her lips parted, as if she wanted to argue the point. But she clamped her mouth closed and held her tongue. As they turned onto the county road heading into town, the silence became rather stilted.

"Ahum, have you noticed many changes in town since you've been back?" he asked.

Faith threw him a startled glance, as if she'd forgotten he was there.

"Um, *ja*, the post office has a new look." She gestured toward the frame building as they drove down Main Street.

He grunted. "They painted it gray last summer. The white trim looks nice."

"And that big sign over Maupin's grocery store is new." She jutted her chin toward the redbrick structure where a large sign spanned the top front of the store in solid black letters.

He nodded and another lengthy hush fell over them.

"Will and Ruth Lapp moved back east last fall," he said.

The Lapps were a young Amish couple with two small children.

"Really? I never thought they would leave here. Where did they go?" she asked.

"Indiana, I think. Will's brother has a large farm there and invited him to go in as partners. Will had been renting his farm here in Colorado. He didn't have enough funds to buy his own place but he had enough to go halves on a large farm with his brother."

"Hmm. That's nice."

He almost laughed out loud. Their dialogue was pretty sad, to say the least. Before Faith left, their exchanges had been long and animated. They'd never had trouble finding topics to discuss. Faith had always been so easy to chat with. So intelligent and filled with life. Now it seemed they had zero to talk about.

"Did you and the bishop have a nice conversation?" he asked.

"Ja," she said, disclosing nothing.

He was dying to ask what they'd talked about but knew that would be more than rude. Hopefully, over time, she'd open up and tell him more about her life and what she'd been doing the past four years.

"*Ach*, have you decided how you're going to decorate your house for Christmas yet?" he asked.

She jerked her head around and stared at him like he'd lost his mind. "Christmas? That's months away. Why would you ask that?"

He shrugged and gave a low chuckle. "Just trying to make conversation."

Her lips twitched, as if she was about to smile. But then she looked away.

"Ah, there it is," he said.

"What?"

He stared straight ahead, focusing on the road. "I knew you could still smile. It was only a matter of time."

She tossed him a shaming frown. "Don't be ridiculous. Of course I can smile. But I doubt we'll be here for Christmas. I'm hoping to leave before the fall harvest."

"Christmas, *Mammi*! Don't wanna leave," Adel said, picking up on their dialogue.

Faith patted her daughter's arm. "Don't you worry, *Liebchen*. We'll celebrate Christmas no matter where we are."

"Ziah be there, too?" Adel asked, leaning her head against his arm.

"Um, he'll be with his own *familye*," Faith said.

Adel frowned but before she could argue the point, Faith lifted her hand and pointed. "Look! We're here."

Josiah pulled into the yard and parked the buggy. After helping the girls down, he glanced at the cemetery surrounded by a low white picket fence.

"They put your *aent* Fern right next to your *onkel*. Do you know the way?" he asked.

Faith nodded. "I could find it in the dark."

She took Adel's hand, walking slowly over the tufts

of uneven grass as they skirted around a perfect line of low, drab headstones.

"Where we go, *Mammi*?" Adel asked.

Josiah could hear Faith's soft voice as she explained who Aunt Fern was and how much she loved the woman. Faith paused beside the dull gray stones and gestured for Adel's benefit, her low voice filled with patience and love. Though he couldn't see Faith's expression, her shoulders trembled and he knew she was crying. She lifted her hand and wiped her eyes, then knelt beside Adel as she wrapped one arm around the child's tiny shoulders and pulled her in close.

Surely Adel was too young to understand what death meant. And Josiah hoped she didn't learn what it was for many years to come. But watching this mother and her child as they knelt beside Fern's and Noah's graves looked so poignant and sad. Faith and Adel had many relatives in the world. Cousins, aunts and uncles, and an entire congregation who cared about them. And yet, they seemed so isolated and remote. Though Josiah was here each day and Bishop Yoder had paid a visit, it appeared that Faith wanted to remain alone. That was completely out of character for the Amish, who shared and did everything together. Even their grief.

Everyone knew Faith had born a child out of wedlock. So, why did she never mention Adel's father? Why was it such a taboo topic? Josiah didn't understand. Not one bit. And once more, he wished she would confide in him, if only to answer the questions burning through his brain and put his mind at ease. But that didn't seem to be something that was ever going to happen. At least, not anytime soon.

Chapter Four

Early Sunday morning, Faith sat on the side of her bed and contemplated staying home from church. The bishop had told her it would be held at his farm. She could probably get away with not going but knew there'd be a price to pay. If she didn't show up, Bishop Yoder would undoubtedly return to the farm looking for her. And because of her religious upbringing, that thought brought her a modicum of shame. She loved *Gott* and had always tried to be faithful and dutiful. But sometimes, her sister's secret was a heavy burden to bear.

Uttering a quiet prayer for help, she determined to cast her troubles on the Lord and do as He would want her to do. She stood and prepared for the day. As she fixed Adel's breakfast, she rehearsed in her mind what she should say. No doubt people would ask where she'd been and why she'd left. Because the tenets of her faith shunned lies, she was determined to speak the truth without revealing anything that might put Adel at risk.

Taking the little girl with her to the barn, Faith set the child on a bale of hay while she fed her aunt's old road horse, Billy. Memories flooded her mind of the many times when Hope had done this chore. She'd always loved this old horse.

The weather was unseasonably warm, the air filled with the fragrance of spring, but Faith took sweaters for her and Adel, just in case. In Colorado, she never knew when the wind would turn cold or a storm might blow in.

"I like Billy," Adel said, holding Martha as she swung her legs back and forth on the bale.

Faith had dressed the child in a clean blue dress, a white cape and apron, and black tights and shoes. She'd tried to pin the girl's wild blond curls back in a little bun beneath her prayer *kapp* but Adel's hair wasn't quite long enough yet.

"I like him, too," Faith said.

As Faith harnessed the elderly animal, she remembered how Hope had frequently offered to feed and groom him.

Tears burned Faith's eyes and she brushed them aside. She'd thought this ancient beast would have died by now. The realization that he was the last livestock her aunt had owned made Faith feel even more melancholy.

When she was ready, she loaded Adel and her dolly, and a small basket containing a loaf of homemade bread and a schnitz apple pie, into the buggy. As she climbed inside, Faith took the leather leads into her hands, released the parking brake and slapped the lines gently against the horse's rump. The buggy lurched forward, the wheels of the contraption rattling over the gravel in the driveway as she headed toward the county road.

"*Mammi*, where we go?" Adel asked, sitting beside her in her child safety seat.

"Where are we going?" Faith corrected the girl's sentence before responding. "We're going to church."

"Ohh," Adel said.

Since they'd actively participated in their cousin's congregation in Akron, Adel knew what to expect. The child gazed out the window, her hands folded quietly around Martha. And in that moment, Faith felt a wave of love and compassion sweep over her. With her head tilted to the side, Adel looked exactly like Hope, and Faith was beyond grateful to have this reminder of her dear sister.

They arrived as the meeting was starting. Faith had timed it just so, in order to avoid as many questions as possible.

A long row of black buggies lined the barbed wire fence surrounding the bishop's hayfield. It looked as though the soil had been plowed but not planted yet.

Faith parked at the end of the row and a teenaged boy ran to help unharness Billy. The animal lifted his head high and swished his tail as the boy turned him loose in the pasture with the other horses. After retrieving Adel and her basket, Faith held the girl's hand as they walked across the lawn toward the heavy timbered barn sitting near the corrals. The beautiful chords of an a cappella hymn rose through the air. They were late but the sermon hadn't started yet.

Stepping inside the barn, Faith glanced around the room, letting her eyes adjust to the dim interior. As was their custom, the men sat facing the women. Faith looked up and caught Josiah's gaze resting heavily on her before he looked away.

To avoid attention, Faith sat near the door on one of the backless benches used specifically for church Sunday. As she settled Adel and her dolly beside her, Faith glanced up and noticed several men and women glancing her way, including the bishop, whose eyes flickered with approval. Ignoring them all, she focused on Adel and started singing, acting as if nothing was out of the ordinary.

The meeting progressed, with a sermon on keeping the Sabbath holy. As she listened to the calming words, Faith felt inspired by a modicum of peace and was glad she'd come. But several times, she found someone in the congregation staring at her. A man or woman, who then leaned close to the person next to them and whispered something in their ear. By the time the service ended, almost all the adults had looked her way and knew she was there.

So much for avoiding attention.

The final prayer was uttered and Faith's courage failed her. She didn't want to stay for lunch. Instead, she picked up Adel and hurried toward the door. The child dropped her doll and Faith whirled around to pick it up.

Sarah Yoder, the bishop's wife, intercepted her. "Faith Mast!"

Too late! Faith was caught.

"*Hallo*, Sarah," Faith said, her heart beating madly in her chest.

The woman embraced her in a tight hug, her voice filled with genuine affection. "How wonderful to see you."

"It's *gut* to see you, too. How is your *familye*?" Faith asked.

Several women and a few men hurried over to her, and Faith quickly found herself surrounded. Her throat felt suddenly dry, like she'd swallowed sandpaper.

"We are *gut*. I'm so glad you're here. I was so happy when Amos told me you'd returned," Sarah said.

Amos was Bishop Yoder, her husband.

"*Danke*. I'm happy to be here, too," Faith said, trying to mean it.

Looking to her right, Faith noticed Josiah's parents standing nearby. John Brenneman listened quietly, his face void of expression. A well-built man with kind eyes that usually flickered with merriment, John was probably what Josiah would look like in thirty more years. But Emma, Josiah's mother, wore an expression of contempt. No doubt she was struggling to forgive Faith for abandoning her son.

Josiah stood leaning against the barn wall, his arms folded, his jaw locked solid as granite. Trina Graber, a girl who had been no more than fourteen when Faith had left, was smiling up at him with adoration. Tossing a challenging glare in Faith's direction, Trina reached up and clasped his arm in a bold statement of possession.

So. It seemed Josiah had a girlfriend after all. Well, good for him.

Aunt Fern had written a year earlier to tell Faith that Josiah was walking out with some of the young women in their congregation. From the looks of things, Trina had staked her claim. And that was fine with Faith. As she turned to face the throng of people, she felt glad for Josiah. He deserved to be happy. He should marry and raise a *familye* of his own. It was time for him to move on and Faith must do the same.

"We were sorry to hear of Hope's passing but we're glad you're back with us now," Norma Albrecht said.

Faith forced her lips to curve in a smile but she didn't speak. The less she said, the better. From what she'd written in her letters, Aunt Fern had told this congregation of Hope's passing, but nothing more. As Faith held Adel against her hip, the child leaned her cheek against her shoulder and gazed shyly at the throng.

"Is this your little girl?" Linda Hostetler asked, reaching up to rub the child's back with the open palm of her hand.

"*Ja*, this is Adel," Faith said.

"*Ach*, your *dochder* is beautiful. She looks just like you. It's a shame Fern never got to meet her," Mercy Lantz said, her voice carrying a note of compassion.

Faith agreed. She hated that Aunt Fern never got to see Adel.

"*Danke*. I wish I could have been here for *Aent* Fern's funeral. I came as soon as I heard of her passing but I won't be staying long."

"*Ach*, why not? You've just returned," Mercy said.

"I plan to sell the farm," Faith said.

This news brought a few startled gasps from the people surrounding her. Saying the words felt so brutal to Faith. It was as if she had announced another death in her family.

"You're going to sell?" Evan Burkholder asked, his voice crowded with disbelief.

"*Ja*, as soon as I find a buyer, Adel and I will be leaving again," Faith said.

There. That was good. News traveled fast among the Amish. By noon tomorrow, everyone in town would know she had a farm to sell, including the *Englisch* population. Hopefully, that would help her find a buyer more quickly.

"If you know of anyone who might be interested in buying, please send them my way," Faith continued.

"*Ach*, your *onkel* Noah would turn over in his grave if he knew you were selling out. A fine farm like that should remain in the *familye*," Evan said, his lips pursed in disapproval.

Knowing he was right, Faith ignored his comment. It couldn't be helped. Her great-uncle Noah would understand and want Adel safe, too.

"Your *aent* never really said where you'd gone off to. She just said you and Hope decided you needed a change of scenery and were living with relatives back east. Exactly where have you been staying all these years?" Mervin Schwartz asked.

There was no censure in his voice, only polite curiosity. But Faith was highly aware that everyone went deathly quiet as they listened for her answer.

"I…I've been living with a widowed *familye* member who needed my help. When Hope got sick and died, I decided to stay," Faith said.

It was the truth, after all. Her distant cousin had her own small farm to look after and Faith had worked hard to assist her in running the place. If Faith didn't return, her cousin would need someone to help her out. Of course, she had numerous relatives living nearby who would see to the task.

"Why have you been gone so long? You never even came home for a visit," Naomi chided.

"And where is your child's *vadder*?" old Marva Geingerich asked.

Well into her nineties, Marva was the matriarch of

the congregation. She glanced around the room with expectation, as though looking for the man.

Faith caught the note of criticism in the elderly woman's tone. When she glanced at Josiah's mother, Faith saw heavy censure in her eyes, too. And Faith couldn't blame her. At one time, she and Josiah had been madly in love. Everyone had known they were going to get married one day. Their families had thought it was a good match and Faith had been great friends with his *mudder*. Though they'd never been formally engaged, everyone had expected it. Faith hated hurting any of them but it couldn't be helped. So much had happened and she and Josiah were different people now. Though he'd expressed his hurt over her leaving, Josiah had apparently recovered and moved on with Trina. Faith hoped his parents could do the same.

"*Ach*, so where is your husband? Why isn't he here?" Marva persisted.

Faith's bravado faltered. A feeling of panic climbed her throat. She couldn't bring herself to tell them she'd never been married. They would only disapprove of her more. Instead, she edged toward the door, hoping to leave. In the process, her heel came down hard on someone's foot and she jerked back.

"I…I'm sorry," she murmured and whirled around, not knowing who she'd stepped on.

Looking up, she saw Josiah. He scowled, his lips drawn tight. In one athletic movement, he shrugged off Trina's hand and took a step toward Faith. For just a moment, she thought he was moving closer to hear her response. Because of their past history, no doubt he disapproved of her more than any.

Before he reached her, Sarah took firm hold of Faith's arm and called out in a loud voice.

"I'm sorry, everyone. But I have an urgent matter I need to speak with Faith about. I've got to take her away from you for a while." Sarah pulled Faith out into the sunshine and toward the clothesline in the backyard.

Carrying Adel and her doll with her, Faith hurried off with the woman, more than grateful to get out of the barn. She glanced over her shoulder at the faces gazing after her but lost sight of Josiah.

Once they were clear of the crowd, Sarah released her arm and stepped back. "I'm sorry to take you away, Faith, but I thought you needed a little space. Are you *allrecht*?"

Releasing a shuddering breath, Faith smiled as she set Adel on her feet. "*Ja*, I'm fine. There's no need to apologize. I…I didn't know how to answer so many questions all at once."

Her hands trembled and she folded her fingers together. Still uncertain of all these strangers, Adel remained nearby but watched the other children with interest as they played in the yard.

"Wh-what was the urgent matter you needed to speak with me about?" Faith asked.

Sarah blinked, as though she couldn't remember. Then… "Um, do you use baking soda when you make your pumpkin bread?"

Faith stared at the woman, stunned by such a flimsy question. And then Faith laughed. Obviously, there was no urgent matter Sarah needed to talk with her about but the woman had to ask her something to account for her real reason in taking Faith away from the mob.

"*Ja*, I most certainly do. Is that the real reason you brought me out here?" Faith asked with a knowing smile.

A flush of red stained Sarah's cheeks. A woman in her early fifties, she tucked a strand of graying hair beneath her starched white prayer *kapp* and gave an uncertain shrug. "In part, but the bishop also asked me to protect you from the barrage of questions he knew you'd be asked about Hope."

Faith tilted her head. "Oh. That was kind of him."

Sarah smiled and squeezed Faith's hand. "He didn't want you to be overwhelmed. We want you and Adel to feel happy and accepted in our *Gmay*. Then, maybe you'll change your mind about selling your farm and decide to stay here with us."

The *Gmay* represented not only a common religious belief in *Gott* but also a system of love and support, no matter what life brought their way. Upon baptism into the faith, each member of the congregation agreed to abide by a specific set of unwritten rules called the *Ordnung*. Like any community, some people were more judgmental than others. Most of these Amish were considerate, kind and compassionate. But some would never approve of Faith, even if they knew the truth and that she was innocent of wrongdoing. In spite of that, the thought of keeping her farm and remaining in Riverton sounded wonderful to Faith, but she knew it wasn't possible. Not as long as there was a chance Brian's parents might guess Adel was their granddaughter.

"I'd best get into the kitchen. Everyone will be wanting their lunch now. Will you join us?" Sarah held an inviting hand toward the farmhouse.

"*Ne*, I…I'm not feeling myself today. I don't think I'm up to it. Maybe next time. But I brought these foods for the noon meal. Will you please give everyone my regrets?" Faith handed Sarah the basket containing the loaf of bread and pie.

Sarah clasped the wicker handle and showed a sympathetic smile. "I understand completely. But remember, it'll get easier. Everyone will talk about your visit today and you won't have to face all their questions next time. The bishop will see to that. Church will be held at the Albrechts' farm in two weeks. The bishop will want to see you there."

Of course he would. Faith merely nodded and watched as Sarah walked away. She knew the bishop would tell the members of the congregation to leave her alone. Bishop Yoder had always been a compassionate man. But regardless of what he said, Faith knew what everyone was thinking. She'd had a child out of wedlock. She wasn't married. A fallen woman. And no decent Amish man would be interested in her now. Which was why she needed the money from the sale of her farm. Going forward, she must have some form of livelihood to support herself and Adel. Only then could she retain her independence. Aunt Fern had undoubtedly realized that. No wonder the woman had left everything to Faith.

"*Mammi*, we go now?" Adel asked, her little forehead curled in a frown.

Picking up the child, Faith headed toward her buggy. "*Ja*, we're going home."

"But wanna play," Adel said, her high forehead furrowed in a scowl as she looked with longing at the laughing children racing across the lawn.

Though she wasn't happy to be leaving, Adel didn't struggle in Faith's arms or throw a tantrum. That just wasn't her way.

Faith hugged the girl and kissed her cheek. "I know, my sweet little dilly bean, but I promise we'll stay next time so you can play. I just don't feel up to it today."

Adel's eyes crinkled with concern. "*Mammi* sick?"

"*Ja, Mammi* is sick at heart today," Faith said.

The girl looked rather sober. "What sick heart?"

Faith shifted the child's weight in her arms and placed her on her feet again. Taking hold of Adel's hand, Faith continued walking as she explained.

"Sick at heart is when you hurt inside right here." Faith placed her free hand over her chest. "There isn't anything wrong with you but you feel sad or upset about something."

"Ohh, like spilling mac-roni," Adel said, twirling one of the ribbons to her prayer *kapp* around her finger.

Faith smiled, remembering the time Adel had disobeyed her and ended up spilling an entire bag of macaroni on the floor. Faith had scolded the child and Adel had felt bad afterward.

"*Ja*, that's right. But when I feel sick at heart, I remember the Savior and I feel calm at heart again," Faith said.

"You calm now?" Adel asked.

Faith nodded. "I feel calmer."

"So, we go back?" Adel asked, turning to look at the children as they chased one another in a game of keep-away.

Faith was half-tempted to return, just to show the judgmental biddies that she wouldn't be defeated. She wanted Adel to feel happy at church. But maybe it was best to avoid the questions and return next time when everyone was over the shock of seeing her again and could remember their manners.

"Not today. But next time, you will play with the children. I promise," Faith said.

The girl accepted this, hopping along as they made their way in silence. Though she was trying hard to have a quiet heart and feel the peace that came with accepting Jesus Christ as her Savior, Faith couldn't help feeling rotten inside. Ever since she'd left town, she'd thought of nothing but returning. Now she wondered if that was a mistake. Instead of sprucing up the farm, maybe she should have stayed in Ohio and hired a real estate agent to bring in workmen to paint and fix the place before selling it for her. Though the agent would undoubtedly take a huge commission, she could have remained in Akron with her memories until it was over with and then use the funds to buy a house of her own. But something had brought her here. The thought of seeing the farm one last time had been like a magnet, pulling her home. And if she was honest with herself, she'd wanted to see Josiah, too. They'd grown apart and he was walking out with other people now, but she'd wanted to look at his face and hear his voice just one last time. And now that was done, she could finally let go for real. Or at least, that's what she told herself.

She'd raise Adel on her own and the child would be safe. Josiah would marry and raise a *familye* with someone else. Once she left town, Faith would never see him again. It was for the best.

So, why did the thought of leaving town cause such an empty ache to fill her heart?

* * *

Josiah tied Faith's road horse to the pasture fence, then stood next to the animal's left front shoulder. Bending at the waist, he ran his hands down the animal's leg until Billy lifted his foot.

As soon as he saw Faith leave the barn following the church service, Josiah had come to the pasture to retrieve her horse for her. Without asking, he knew she wanted to go home. Obviously, the barrage of questions from members of their congregation had been too much for her and he didn't understand why. If she didn't want to live in Riverton anymore, why didn't she just tell everyone that? Why did she seem so evasive?

When she'd first left town four years earlier, Fern told everyone that she and Hope had wanted a fresh start elsewhere and they were staying with *familye*. Everyone assumed he and Faith had had a falling-out. And since they'd argued before she left, Josiah accepted that. But why was Faith so skittish now when asked about Adel's father? Why didn't she just tell everyone who the man was? Her reticence must be caused by shame and embarrassment. After all, she'd had a child out of wedlock. That was a major taboo for the Amish but it wasn't unheard of. And it certainly wasn't Adel's fault. Yet, Josiah sensed there was something else going on here. Something he didn't understand.

With Adel to look after, Faith had her hands full, so Josiah thought he'd harness Billy for her. But when he retrieved the animal from the pasture, he noticed Billy was limping heavily.

Hurrying to his own buggy, Josiah retrieved a small toolbox his father kept there for just such problems. Returning to Billy, Josiah leaned over and held the gelding's foot with his left hand to inspect the hoof.

Yep, Billy had thrown a shoe.

Using a pick, Josiah cleaned out the dirt and manure on both sides of the horse's frog, around the sole and through both bars of the hoof. As he worked, he inspected the area for any small stones, bruising, cracks or foul odors. One nail still protruded from the hoof and Josiah used a crease nail puller to remove it.

"What are you doing?"

Startled, Josiah jerked, then looked up and saw Faith and Adel standing off to one side.

"Your horse has thrown a shoe. I was taking a look to ensure he didn't have a worse problem," Josiah said, turning back to his work.

Billy blew dust from his nostrils. A swish of long lavender skirts swirled beside Josiah as Faith came to stand nearby. Without looking up, Josiah was conscious of her leaning over to inspect his work.

"Do you think it's serious? Is he lame?" Faith asked.

Josiah caught her fresh, clean scent and took a deep inhale before placing the horse's foot on the ground and standing up straight. He would have moved away but the body of the horse blocked his escape. Instead, he found himself gazing into Faith's brilliant blue eyes.

"*Ne*, um, I think he's *allrecht*. We caught it in time. But I wouldn't make him pull your buggy home today," he said, feeling suddenly out of sorts.

Faith stepped away and he released a breath, more than relieved to put some distance between them. He didn't know what was wrong with him. There was no logical reason for him to be nervous around Faith and he told himself it was just because he no longer loved her.

"Billy hurt?" Adel asked, gazing at the horse with worry.

"*Ja*, Billy's hurt. But he's going to be okay," Faith reassured her daughter. Then the woman glanced at Josiah. "But how will we get home? It's too far for us to walk."

In places like Indiana and Lancaster County, many Amish farms were located close together, within walking distance. But here in Colorado, they were spread miles and miles apart.

He shrugged one shoulder. "I'll borrow a horse from the bishop. Give me a few minutes to go and tell him what's happened. Then, I'll harness the animal, drive you and Adel home, and ride the horse back here to the bishop's farm. I can return in time to catch a ride home with my parents later this afternoon."

Now, why had he offered to do that? Josiah didn't know. But in his heart, he knew it was the right thing to do. He didn't love Faith but she and Adel still needed a way home. He couldn't abandon them in their time of need, no matter what. The Savior had taught him that much.

"But you'll miss your lunch," Faith said.

"I don't think I'll starve. I can grab something to eat once I return."

He waited patiently, giving her time to consider her options. From the reticence in her eyes, he could tell she wasn't prepared to return to the bishop's house and all the curious looks and questions thrown her way. And since the bishop's place was a good five miles outside of town, Josiah doubted she'd want to make

Adel walk that far. She could borrow a horse from the bishop and drive herself home, but then she'd need to figure out a way to return the animal. And with Billy lame, she couldn't do that easily. Not without help.

"*Allrecht, danke* for your offer," she finally said, her voice laced with hesitancy.

Turning, he took off at a sprint, racing back to the bishop's yard, where long tables covered by white butcher paper had been set out for the noon meal. The men were just taking their seats, the women carrying large platters of sliced ham and homemade bread, bowls of potato salad, and other yummy food out of the house to set before them. Josiah knew the men would be fed first, then the children and women. For several hours, they'd all visit, gossip about Faith and her daughter, then retire to their homes before nightfall. In two weeks, they'd do it all over again. Except they'd hopefully drop the topic of Faith and Adel by that time.

With a quick explanation, Josiah told the bishop of the problem, received permission to borrow a horse, then hurried back to Faith. As he passed by the tables, Sarah Yoder shot out a hand to stop him.

"*Ach*, I take it you're driving Faith and Adel *heemet*?" she asked.

He nodded. "Her horse is lame."

"Then, you'll need something to eat. Take this with you." Sarah handed him a plate piled high with ham and cheese sandwiches and chocolate chip cookies she'd quickly assembled right there on the spot.

"*Danke!*" he called over his shoulder as he hurried away.

Faith looked startled when he handed her the plate and explained who had given it to him.

"That was kind of Sarah," Faith said.

They paused a moment to offer a silent blessing on the food, then Faith handed Adel a wedge of sandwich. The girl smiled her gratitude and bit into the soft bread, meat and cheese while Josiah retrieved one of the bishop's horses from the pasture. Within minutes, he had the animal harnessed to Faith's buggy, Billy tied to the back, and they were on their way. As Josiah held the leads and drove the bishop's horse with one hand, Faith placed a sandwich in his free hand. They ate along the way. Because Josiah didn't want to push Billy too hard, he drove slowly. The rhythmic clip-clop of the bishop's horse was restive and little Adel soon fell asleep, laying her head in her mommy's lap.

"You know, Billy is quite old now. He ought to be retired. I could sell him and purchase a younger road horse for you to drive," Josiah suggested before biting into a cookie.

Faith gazed at him for several moments, seeming to contemplate his offer. "I definitely need a road horse while I'm here but I hate to buy an expensive animal before I leave."

Glancing her way, he saw the consternation on her face.

"I could lend you one of my road horses," he said.

She lifted her eyebrows in question. "You own more than one?"

He nodded. "*Ja*, I raise and train them to sell. Once I buy my own farm, I hope to continue doing so. It's a lucrative side business that allows me to work full-time on my farm instead of taking a secondary job, too."

"*Ach*, you always were extra *gut* with horses and I

know you wanted to raise and sell them as part of your livelihood. I'm glad you've met that goal," she said.

She didn't sound surprised and he realized they'd once known so much about each other. They'd made so many plans together. But now, he felt so distant from this woman. Like they were almost strangers.

"I mostly sell to other Amish within our community but I've shipped a few horses back east, too. It's provided me with a nice savings account to put a large deposit on my own farm one day. My horses are *gut* and gentle. That's how I train them," he said.

"I'm surprised you don't have your own farm already," she said.

He shrugged. "There was no reason to leave my parents' place."

He made the admission reluctantly and wished he'd bought his own farm. For some odd reason, he hated her to know that he still lived at home with his folks. If Faith had stayed in Riverton, they would have been married and had their own place by now. He might have even bought Fern's farm and just moved in with her. Since the elderly lady needed care, the situation would have been ideal. But they couldn't go back in time and there was no sense in contemplating it now.

"I'd be honored to rent one of your horses while I'm in town but I don't want to sell Billy," Faith said.

"Then, what will you do with him?"

"Put him out to pasture."

He blinked at that. What an absurd idea. For the Amish, their livestock were a tool they used to work their farms, just like a rake, hoe or baler. As a general rule, they didn't have pets or waste time feeding livestock that didn't earn their keep. Even their cats and dogs were used for catching mice and herding sheep or goats.

"Why would you keep a broken-down old horse that can't work the land anymore?" he asked.

Faith turned to stare out the window but not before he caught the shimmer of tears in her cerulean eyes. "Because Hope loved Billy. She always had a tender spot for him. I don't want him to end up as dog food or at a glue factory in Mexico."

Josiah frowned. Her sister again. Even when they'd been little girls, Faith was always looking after Hope, always putting her sister's wants and needs above her own. And although Hope was gone now, it appeared Faith's feelings hadn't changed one bit.

"But you're selling your farm. No buyer is going to want to keep Billy around once you leave," he said.

She lifted her stubborn chin at least two inches higher in the air and wore that tenacious expression she always had when she was determined to get her way. "Then, I'll make it part of the agreement that Billy gets to live the rest of his life out in the pasture. If the new buyer won't agree, I won't sell the farm to them."

Really? He could hardly believe she'd insist on such an insane stipulation. Surely she wouldn't jeopardize the sale of her property over such a trivial issue. But this was Faith he was talking to. Always sweet, gentle and kind…unless her loyalty was tested. She was fiercely protective. In the past, Josiah knew this woman had a spine of steel and a will of iron. Where her *familye* and faith in *Gott* were concerned, she never backed down and never gave in. But apparently he'd been wrong about that too, since she'd had a child out of wedlock.

"You can do as you like. I'll bring one of my road horses over to your place first thing tomorrow morning," he said.

She nodded and they didn't speak much as he turned onto the graveled road leading to her farmhouse. After all, it wasn't his business what she did with her old road horse. Other than working on her farm and being a member of her congregation, he wasn't part of her life now. Even if he were, he would never think of telling her what to do. Not with her own horse.

Pulling up beside her white frame house, he hopped out and gently lifted Adel out of her child safety seat. He stood there waiting, holding the sleeping child in his arms as Faith preceded him up the cobbled walk path to the front door. He followed her inside, to the little girl's bedroom where he laid her carefully on the bed, then stood back. As Adel rolled onto her side, Faith covered her tiny form with a warm blanket. Josiah returned to the living room and reached for the doorknob, hesitating as Faith joined him there.

"*Danke* for seeing us safely home," she said, laying her and Adel's gray sweaters on the sofa.

"You're *willkomm*. I'll put your buggy in the barn and see to Billy before I return to the bishop's farm. I'll see you tomorrow," he said, opening the door.

She nodded and turned away, dismissing him. As he stepped outside onto the front porch, Josiah closed the door quietly behind him. He returned to the buggy and drove it into the barn, feeling rather odd. He unhitched the bishop's horse from the contraption and put Billy in a stall, ensuring the elderly beast had plenty of water. Then, he saddled the bishop's equine and rode the animal back to the bishop's farm. By the time he arrived, lunch was over with and his father was helping the bishop and several other men load the long tables into the enclosed wagon that carried them and the backless benches to each farm for their church meetings.

Trina Graber stood in the front yard, craning her neck toward him. When he rode up and hopped down off the horse, she hurried over and took hold of his arm. He felt a strong urge to shrug her off. Instead, he tried to smile politely and responded to her dialogue about the quilt she was planning to make with her mother. He'd courted Trina a couple of times but she seemed much more taken with him than he was with her. In fact, as he carefully disengaged his arm from her hand, he thought it had been a mistake to have ever asked her out. She was just too young and puerile for him.

"I think I'd better help the men," he said, finding a legitimate excuse to get away from her cloying fingers.

"*Ach*, okay. I'll see you later."

She waved and backed away and he hated to hurt her feelings. But he disliked leading her on when there wasn't anything there. She just wasn't what he was looking for in a bride. She was attractive enough but he didn't find her dark brown hair and eyes as appealing as other girls he'd spent time with.

What was he thinking? He'd only walked out with one girl with blond hair and blue eyes, and her name was Faith Mast. But that had ended years ago. She would sell her farm and leave the area soon. He'd probably never see her again. And that was for the best. Because he was finished with her for good.

Chapter Five

"*Mammi!* *Mammi*, see!"

Faith heard Adel's cry of delight all the way in the back of the house. Having just finished making the beds, Faith hurried down the hallway to the living room, where she found the child standing on the sofa as she held on to Martha and bounced up and down. Early-morning sunlight bathed the wide picture window in a golden haze as the girl pointed with enthusiasm.

Driving a horse and buggy, Josiah's father came down the lane and pulled into the front yard. A beautiful young standardbred bay gelding was tied to the back of the buggy. Head held high, dark mane flowing against its neck, the animal trotted along at a fast clip. The entourage didn't stop but continued on past the house.

Behind his father, Josiah drove his own horse and buggy with two enormous Percheron draft horses tied at the back and bringing up the rear. The gigantic prancing beasts presented quite a parade as they lumbered by and headed toward the corrals.

What on earth was going on?

"Ziah here. Ziah here." Dressed in her white prayer *kapp* and a simple blue dress, Adel waved Martha in excitement before jumping off the couch and sprinting toward the back door with bare feet.

Hurrying after the child, Faith called to the girl. "Adel! Wait!"

Adel did as told, stopping obediently at the end of the rock path that meandered across the back lawn. Her small body vibrated with energy as Martha dangled from her hand. Faith didn't want her to race headlong into all those flying hooves.

When Faith reached the graveled driveway, she picked up the child and doll and carried them across the sharp gravel. For the life of her, Faith couldn't imagine why Josiah had brought so many horses to her place. She'd expected one road horse.

John Brenneman, Josiah's father, stood untying the standardbred from the back of his buggy. At the age of fifty-three, John was still lean and strong, his bushy beard a mixture of brown and gray. When he saw Faith, he tugged respectfully on the brim of his straw hat, then led the horse over to the hitching post.

"Guder mariye." John spoke low, his eyes and voice carrying a hint of reticence.

At one time, John had been more than friendly and had spoken to Faith with exuberance. But after her sudden departure four years earlier, she couldn't blame him for being cautious around her now.

"Gut morning," she returned, trying to be pleasant. After all, it wasn't his fault that she appeared to be a fallen woman.

Like his wife, no doubt John disapproved of her now.

For that matter, her entire congregation must believe the worst about her. How she longed to tell them it wasn't true. She'd kept the faith. But even if she hadn't, wasn't she still deserving of empathy and love? It had actually been Hope who'd violated the tenets of their *Ordnung*. But even so, Hope deserved to be treated with compassion, too.

Turning to face Josiah, Faith brushed away her gloomy thoughts. Soon she'd sell the farm and move far away. She'd be back with her cousin's Amish congregation in Ohio, where they knew the truth. What these Amish in Riverton thought of her wouldn't matter anymore. And yet, it mattered to her. A lot.

Josiah hopped out of his buggy and circled around to see to the tall Percherons. Still clasping Adel's hand, Faith went after him, keeping her distance from the plate-sized hooves of the big horses.

"Why did you bring the Percherons?" she asked, unable to hide her surprise.

He barely spared her a glance as he ran his hand down the neck of one gray horse. "To plow your barley fields, of course. Remember, we discussed that you wanted me to turn over the weeds and plant a crop this year? And you don't have any horses."

"Oh. *Ja*, of course."

She hadn't forgotten but neither had she thought it through. *Onkel* Noah or an Amish man hired by *Aent* Fern had always plowed their fields. She hadn't worried about it. Josiah needed strong horses to accomplish the task. But she'd never expected him to bring his own horses to work her farm. Realizing he couldn't do the chore without the labor of strong beasts, she felt rather foolish.

Adel squirmed in her arms, so Faith set the child down. The dirt was soft here and wouldn't injure the girl's feet.

"Hi, Ziah," Adel called, a smile brightening her little face as she squashed Martha close against her chest.

Leading one of the big grays over to the corral, Josiah tied the animal to the fence, then turned and smiled wide.

"*Ach, hallo*, dilly bean. How are you today?" he asked.

"Fine," she said, her voice high and sweet. "What their name?" she asked, pointing at the draft horses.

Josiah reached out and caressed first one horse's neck, then the other's. "This one is Jack and this is Tilly."

"Jack and Tilly," Adel repeated, smiling at the large animals.

"Tilly's going to foal sometime in the fall but I can still work her for now," he said.

Adel tilted her head to one side. "Foal?"

"She's going to have a *boppli*."

"Ohh." Adel nodded in understanding, hugging her dolly tighter.

Josiah picked up the child and swung her around. Adel dropped her doll as she held tightly to his arms and laughed out loud. Picking up the doll and brushing the dirt off her miniature dress, Faith stared at the girl, wondering at her joyous transition.

"Did I hear someone over here is called dilly bean?" John asked with incredulity as he came to lean against the fence.

Dressed just like his son in black broadfall pants,

work boots and a blue chambray shirt, the man pushed his straw hat back on his forehead as he smiled wide.

"*Ja*, that me," Adel cried.

As Josiah set her on her feet, the little girl glanced between the two men and grinned.

"What kind of name is that for a little *maedel*?" John reached down and tickled the child's ribs.

Adel squealed with delight, her giggles filling the air. Seeing the child so happy did something to Faith inside. She couldn't remember ever seeing Adel this animated. They'd had horses, cows, goats, pigs and chickens on their cousin's farm. The child had interacted with them all on a daily basis. But since they'd moved here, a change had come over the girl. Faith couldn't put her finger on what had made the difference. She was grateful John seemed to hold no grudge against her child. Being here was temporary and Faith decided to enjoy her brief visit home and smiled, too.

"*Ach*, my fields aren't going to plow themselves. I'll leave you to it and be on my way." With a nod at Josiah, John stepped toward his waiting buggy.

Faith smiled her gratitude. "*Danke* for your help, John."

He glanced at her over his shoulder and tugged on the brim of his straw hat but didn't speak.

"I'll see you tonight at supper," Josiah called after his father's retreating back.

"Where John go?" Adel asked, watching the older man as he climbed inside his buggy and slapped the leads against the horse's rump.

"He's got his own work to do, dilly. But you'll see him again at church in a couple weeks," Josiah said. "Now, would you like to meet your new road horse?"

Adel nodded eagerly as John's buggy rattled away and turned onto the lane leading to the county road. Josiah led Adel over to where the bay gelding stood dozing in the warm sunshine. Faith followed, feeling grateful for the use of his Percherons. She folded her arms as she watched her child interact with the road horse. Lifting the girl up, Josiah let her rub the animal's velvety nose and black mane. The horse's coat gleamed, absolutely beautiful.

"This mine?" Adel asked, her voice filled with awe.

Ah-hah! Now Faith understood Adel's excitement. In Ohio, all the livestock had belonged to her cousin Sadie. But here, it was obvious Adel felt like this was her home and these animals belonged to her. Somehow, even in her young mind, Adel understood the difference. Faith felt the same way and she couldn't deny how good it was to be home, if only for a short while.

Josiah tossed a hesitant glance at Faith. "*Ja*, he is your horse. I am gifting him to you."

"Oh! Mine," Adel whispered in awe. She hopped up and down and clapped her hands with excitement.

"Ach, ne!" Faith said. "This is a lovely, expensive animal. You've undoubtedly spent hours training this horse to do his work. You should keep him for yourself or sell him and make a profit."

Josiah threw her a shaming glance. "You know profit isn't everything. And I have several road horses. This is between your *dochder* and me. I'm giving Adel a gift. I want her to have this horse and I hope you won't interfere."

What could Faith say to that? Though they'd be leaving town soon, she wasn't about to argue the point. Adel looked so jubilant. How could Faith steal this happy moment from her? But even worse, how could Faith make Adel leave her horse behind when they finally left town? They wouldn't be able to take the animal with them. Not all the way to Ohio. In the end, the horse would undoubtedly be returned to Josiah.

A sigh of frustration escaped Faith's lips. Adel blinked in wonderment and gazed at the animal's big brown eyes.

"What will you name him?" Josiah said.

The girl tilted her head to one side and pressed a finger to her chin, as if thinking this over...a gesture she had learned from Faith. Finally, Adel spoke with a decisive nod of her head. "His name Bean!"

Josiah chuckled. "Bean? You really want to name him that?"

Adel nodded in finality. "*Ja*, his name Bean."

"His name *is* Bean." Faith corrected the girl's grammar in *Deitsch*.

Faith stepped over and patted the horse's withers. If she was going to be caring for this animal and harnessing him to her buggy all the time, she'd better get to know him, too.

"I think Bean is a fine name," Josiah said, looking at her.

"*Ach*, it's as good as any," Faith agreed.

Except that this horse was special because he now belonged to Adel and she had named him.

"*Ach*, I'd best get to work. I've got the barley fields to plow and I'm hoping to finish them this week." Josiah glanced at the clear sky.

Faith knew he was tracking the movement of the sun. It was a habit of all farmers. She knew he'd spent valuable time bringing the horses to her farm but it couldn't be helped.

As he sauntered away, she wondered how she could repay him for the use of his animals. As he headed toward the barn, she noticed his empty hands. Usually, he packed a personal-sized red cooler chest with his lunch inside. Obviously he hadn't packed one today. Or maybe he'd forgotten and left it at home. Either way, Faith knew he'd work long, hard hours and go hungry without something to eat at midday.

Hmm. Maybe she could prepare a meal and take it out to the fields to him later on. It didn't have to be a big deal. Just a kind gesture to thank him for everything he'd done for them.

She would pack a small cooler chest for her and Adel, too. Except they would go elsewhere and enjoy a little picnic, just the two of them. That would be fun for Adel. The child was getting way too attached to Josiah anyway, a problem that was now complicated with her horse, Bean. Spending extra time with Josiah and the new road horse would only make things more difficult when it came time for Faith to sell the farm and leave town.

No matter what, Faith and Adel were not staying here in Riverton. It might be difficult, but when the time came, Faith would pack up her little girl and they would go far away where they'd be safe. Adel would soon get over missing the farm, Bean and Josiah. And so would Faith. At least, that's what Faith hoped.

Josiah took a deep, settling breath. Driving the old wheel-mounted sulky plow that Faith's great-uncle Noah had used for years, Josiah raised the hand lever and lowered it for the umpteenth time. A small wave of dust settled over him and he held his breath and turned his face away until it passed. This riding plow was easier to manage and required less strength to control the depth and direction of the furrow than a walking one, but it was still archaic and much slower than using a newer model like his father's four-bottom plow. Thankfully the sulky at least had two shares and was capable of cultivating in both directions. Otherwise, tilling Faith's barley fields would take forever to complete. And Josiah was anxious to get it planted and move on to the next chore.

He didn't begrudge the work. In fact, he felt good to finally be plowing these fields. They'd lain fallow for years. And it could be worse. He could be driving a walking moldboard plow. Also, if these fields had too many stones in them, he would have had to remove the seat and walk behind the horses, to pick up the rocks. But before his death, Noah had farmed this land for years, leaving the soil nicely broken. Josiah just wished Noah hadn't been so frugal and had bought a better plow.

The contraption suddenly jerked and tilted. Once again, the share hit a large mound of earth and jumped the furrow. Fighting to keep his balance, Josiah heaved a disgruntled sigh and righted the wheels before straightening out his Percherons. In addition to his father's four-bottom plow, maybe Josiah should have borrowed several of his father's horses, too. Then, Josiah could finish this chore within two days. But his father needed his tools to till his own fields. And since it did no good begrudging Noah's ancient equipment, Josiah resigned himself to working with what he had. But if Josiah owned this fine farm, he'd immediately invest in a newer plow and at least four more draft horses.

Coming to the end of the row, Josiah turned the two Percherons.

"Gee! Get up!" he called, swerving the horses to the right.

A movement over by the house caught Josiah's eye and he looked up. Faith was walking toward him, carrying a large wicker basket and holding Adel's hand as the child hopped happily over each hill of freshly turned sod.

"Woah!" Josiah pulled Jack and Tilly to a halt.

He secured the traces and hopped down off the plow seat. Standing at seventeen hands high and weighing around two thousand pounds each, the Percherons were well-muscled with large, intelligent eyes and gentle manners. But they'd been working hard that morning and were fidgety.

Jack swung his great head and tugged against his bridle. Tilly stamped her hooves, seeming eager to finish the row. The two animals knew their work wasn't done. So the horses' movements wouldn't frighten Adel, Josiah placed himself between them as Faith came to a stop nearby.

"Hallo!" he greeted them in a friendly tone.

"Hi, Ziah," Adel returned, waving one hand.

"Hi, sweetie. What brings you out my way?" he asked.

Faith indicated the wicker basket, a guarded wariness filling her beautiful blue eyes. "Um, we're going to have ourselves a picnic over by the stream. Since I noticed you didn't have your cooler chest with you this morning, I thought maybe we could drop off some food for you first."

How thoughtful of her. But Faith had always been

like that. Polite and considerate. Until she'd abandoned him.

He lifted his hands to his hips and considered the woman and child for several moments. "That's nice of you. Mind if I join you by the stream?"

The moment the question left his mouth, he regretted it. Faith frowned and stepped back, looking nervous. She obviously didn't want him tagging along. But since Cherry Creek meandered across the entire length of her property, it was only a stone's throw away. What was she going to do, sit beside the stream and eat with Adel while he sat here on the plow seat alone?

"I need to water my horses anyway. But I can't dally very long. I've got a lot to do," he said, speaking the truth.

In fact, the less time he spent with this woman, the better. She had broken his heart. She'd left him high and dry without a single word. Then, she'd taken up with some stranger, getting herself caught with a child out of wedlock. Josiah longed to know who the man was. And why wasn't the guy here with his *familye* now? But one thing was for sure. Josiah couldn't trust Faith again. It'd be best if he kept his distance. Of course, Adel was another matter. He adored the little girl and loved being near her. Her innocence and guileless manners reminded him of Faith long ago, before she'd become jaded by the world.

"I, um, sure," Faith said. "You can join us. We won't be out here long, either. I've got lye water cooling on the back porch. I've dug out my aunt's molds and am making a batch of soap later this afternoon. And just in the nick of time. I'm almost out."

He nodded. Both of them were busy, like a normal *familye*. Except they weren't. A *familye*, that is.

"*Allrecht*, I'll join you in just a minute. Let me take care of my horses first," he said.

Lifting the plow blade, he led the big animals over to the stream, where they drank deeply. Then, he put them to rest beneath the sheltering shade of a tall cottonwood tree. The two beasts immediately lowered their heads to crop grass.

By the time Josiah joined the girls, Faith had spread a thin blanket along the embankment and laid out a plastic container of ham and cheese sandwiches, potato salad, apple slices and homemade brownies.

"All ready," Faith said.

On her cue, Josiah lowered his head and they said a silent blessing on the food. Then, Faith offered half a sandwich to Adel. The girl took a bite right out of the middle, chewing happily. She didn't even try to take a brownie. Not until she'd finished her sandwich and two pieces of apple. Josiah figured that was a lot of food for a little girl.

"May I have a brownie, please?" Adel asked her mother.

"Of course." Faith smiled as she presented the treat to the child.

"Can I walk along the stream?" Adel asked.

Looking uneasy, Faith glanced at the ditch. She undoubtedly noticed how deep and swift the water was. "*Ja*, but don't get in the water and stay nearby so I can see you at all times."

"I will, *Mammi*."

The girl hurried along the embankment, taking bites

of her brownie from time to time. She tossed a rock into the water and laughed.

"She's happy today," Josiah remarked.

"She's always happy but more so since I brought her home," Faith said.

He took a bite of sandwich. "Why do you think that is?"

She shrugged. "Who knows? Maybe it's because she knows this farm is ours. Maybe it's because you gave her a horse."

She tossed a half-exasperated look in his direction and he laughed.

"She has Hope's eyes. Pale blue, like a robin's egg," he said.

She jerked and blinked at him, her sandwich held in midair. "That's an odd thing to say."

He took a big swallow of lemonade. "Not really. You two were identical but I could always tell you apart just by looking at your eyes. Since you were twins, I suppose it's logical that your *dochder* inherited your sister's eyes. Other than that, Adel looks just like you."

She glanced down, her sandwich forgotten. "I…I suppose so."

They were quiet a moment, both lost in their own thoughts. Finally, they started eating again. The trickling of the stream and rustling of the trees overhead felt so restive. This was a beautiful, idyllic place. For a few moments, Josiah could almost pretend this was his *familye*. That they all belonged to each other.

Then, reality intruded.

"Who is her *vadder*?" he asked.

Faith choked on a bite of sandwich. He patted her

back, watching her expression as she coughed hard. The tranquil moment was broken.

"Are you *allrecht*?" he asked.

"*Ja*, it just went down the wrong pipe."

He gave her a moment to recover, then asked again the question that had been burning a hole in his brain.

"Who is Adel's *vadder*?"

"I…I would rather not say. It's not something I want to discuss," she said.

Even though they weren't finished eating, she started gathering up the picnic to leave. Realizing he was losing her, he changed the topic.

"Have you decided on a price for your farm yet?" he asked.

She hesitated, gazing at him with wide, uncertain eyes. "*Ach*, I don't know. I don't even have any idea what the place is worth. I'd have to ask a real estate agent in town for help. Why do you ask?"

He took a brownie from its plastic container before she slid the lid on top. "I'd like to buy it from you. I was wondering if, once you know your asking price, would you give me first dibs at purchasing the place?"

She sat back and went very still, her gaze locked on him. "You…you want to buy my farm?"

He nodded. "*Ja*, I do very much. It has nice, fertile land and water and I'd take *gut* care of it."

She turned away. "I know you would."

"I'd like to live here. It's a beautiful farm," he said.

She looked up, her eyes filled with a wistfulness he didn't understand. "*Ja*, it certainly is. I wish I didn't have to sell."

"So, why don't you stay? Why do you have to leave?"

Placing the rest of the containers inside the wicker

basket, she wouldn't meet his eyes. "My life is elsewhere now. Adel and I don't belong here anymore. But I'll definitely give you the first option to buy the place. I think *Aent* Fern and *Onkel* Noah would have loved for you to live here. They always liked you. And I know you'd always take *gut* care of things."

Her vote of confidence touched him like nothing else could. But as she packed up their lunch and stepped away, Josiah was filled with misgivings.

"Adel, *komm* on, *Liebchen*. We've got to go home now."

"Ah, wanna stay," Adel cried, though she came obediently.

"I know, sweetums. But I've still got soap to make. Our fun picnic must *komm* to an end."

"Allrecht." The child acquiesced but her voice was filled with disappointment.

"Bye, Ziah." Adel waggled her fingers at him.

He waved back. "*Mach's gut*, sweetie. I'll see you tomorrow."

Watching them walk back to the farmhouse, Josiah's mind was filled with confusion. Faith's apprehension when he mentioned Adel's father had not escaped his notice. He realized Faith was frightened by something, or someone. And for the life of him, he couldn't understand who or what.

Chapter Six

By the end of the following week, Josiah had planted the barley and spread compost on Faith's garden plot. The late-April weather had provided a heavy rain shower the night before. This morning, the air was warm and clear and smelled of washed earth and sage. It was time for Faith to plant carrots, beets, radishes, squash and a variety of other vegetables.

But why?

Walking outside, she crossed the barnyard, stepping over puddles that dotted the graveled yard. She couldn't explain her desire to grow a garden this season. Not when she wouldn't be here for the harvest. She and Adel would be long gone before the autumn frosts covered the land. She definitely wouldn't be around to bottle the produce.

Or would she?

With all the work they were doing to spruce up the farm, if she left before it was sold, the place would fall right back into disrepair. What if Josiah couldn't afford her asking price? What if she couldn't sell the place?

Shaking her head, she thrust aside her pessimistic

thoughts. She must have faith in *Gott*. Over the past few years, she'd felt so alone. But the Lord had never abandoned her. Deep within her heart, she knew He'd been there, watching over her and Adel. Still, the thought of planting a garden and then leaving it behind upset her more than she could say. Perhaps it was because of her upbringing. Growing a garden and bottling the produce had been ingrained in her since she was born. It flowed within her blood. Without preserving food during times of plenty, her *familye* would have faced hunger in the coming winter months.

Maybe she should offer to let the Amish women in her congregation pick her produce for themselves. Then, the food wouldn't go to waste. Of course, once she sold the place, Faith wouldn't be here to let them in. But she sure couldn't stand to leave the land fallow while she lived here, either. The greenery would undoubtedly help show the farm better to a potential buyer. And the work would keep her occupied, too. She certainly couldn't sit idle while she waited for a sale.

Heading toward the barn, she looked around for Josiah. She'd seen him climbing on a ladder earlier that morning to replace the roof to the chicken coop and make repairs. It would be nice when he finished, but it saddened her heart that she had no chickens on the place.

As she came around the corner, she bumped smack into his solid chest.

"Oof!" he grunted and dropped a hammer before reaching out to steady her.

"*Ach*, I'm sorry," she cried, backing up quick.

He laughed and released his hold on her arm, but not

before she felt the warm strength of his hand against her skin.

"Where are you going in such a hurry?" he asked, his eyes flashing with merriment as his handsome lips curved in a smile.

She couldn't meet his eyes as she fidgeted with a string on her prayer *kapp.* "I…I wanted to let you know I'll be driving into town. I need to speak with the Realtor and also buy some garden seeds and tomato plants. Can I pick up any supplies for you while I'm there?"

He nodded readily. "*Ja,* I need another bale of chicken wire and several two-by-fours to finish my repairs. That's a bit much for you to carry. Maybe I could ride along?"

She hesitated, wishing she hadn't told him of her plans. It was on the tip of her tongue to ask him to go into town without her but she really needed to meet with the real estate agent. That was something she must do herself.

"Of course you can ride with me," she said.

He brushed a smattering of sawdust off his pants. "I'm at a standstill in my work and can go anytime you're ready."

She glanced at the house. "Adel should be waking up from her nap. Give me a few minutes to get her ready and we can go."

"*Gut!* I'll harness Jack to the wagon and meet you out front."

She glanced at the barn. "The wagon? We can't take the buggy?"

"*Ne,* we'll need the wagon to carry the boards and bale of wire."

She nodded, grateful he was there to do the restorations. Most Amish men were skilled carpenters and builders. Without his expertise, she wouldn't have a clue.

"Then, we'll take the wagon. Is it a big repair job?" she asked.

"*Ne*, it's no big deal. Once we return, I'll have it fixed within an hour or so. Then, you can put chickens in the coop anytime you like."

How she would love to buy some chickens. She'd always loved the fluffy baby chicks. And the birds provided many benefits to a farm. Not only did they give eggs and meat but they also ate bugs that would otherwise infest her garden and flower beds.

"Um, do you think it unwise for me to buy some baby chicks for the coop?" she finally asked.

"Of course not. That would be a fine idea," Josiah said, his voice filled with exuberance.

His optimism lifted her spirits a bit. "But what will I do with them once I sell the farm? I can't very well take them with me."

He shrugged those wide shoulders of his. "Leave them here. You can always include any of your livestock in the sale of the farm. I'll have the coop finished before I leave to go home this evening. Why don't we pick up the chicks today, along with some feed?"

She glanced at the pristine sky, knowing it could rain or send a chilling frost any day now. "You don't think it's too cold for chicks?"

He shook his head. "*Ne*, the weather is warming up nicely and they'll be laying eggs for you within five months."

Five months. For a farmer, that was such a short time. But that would take them into the autumn months.

She didn't want to be here for Thanksgiving and Christmas. Celebrating the holidays here at the farm would only make it more difficult to leave when the time came.

"I suppose I could keep the babies in a box beside the woodstove in my kitchen, just for a week or so, until there's no chance of a frost and they get some size to them," she said.

"*Ja*, they'll grow fast. My *mamm* keeps our new chicks by the stove, too."

She looked at the coop, thinking they sounded like an old married couple, talking things over, making plans for their farm. But they weren't a couple. They never could be again.

"Okay, I'll buy some chicks today, too," she said.

"*Gut!* I'll meet you out front in a few minutes." He flashed a smile so bright she had to blink.

As he turned and walked toward the barn, she stared after him. His solid arms swung freely at his sides, his stride filled with the energy of a strong, confident man. Though they were no longer going together and he was seeing someone else, he inspired Faith with confidence.

As she returned to the house, she realized Josiah was delighted by her decision to buy the chicks. And for some crazy reason, pleasing him made Faith feel happy, too. It was just because she loved baby chickens and was eager to see livestock on the farm again. Wasn't it?

If it took her a long time to sell the farm, she'd need the meat and eggs, too. And yet, it was something more. Something she couldn't quite put her finger on. Putting chickens in the coop Josiah was repairing felt like a partnership with him. And that didn't make sense. Because they weren't partners. No, not at all.

Inside the house, Adel had just awoken from her nap. Looking a bit disoriented, she stood barefoot in the kitchen. Martha hung limp from one of her tiny hands as she rubbed her eyes with the other. Upon seeing Faith, Adel immediately reached out for her. Faith picked up the child and sat on a chair, hugging her close.

"*Hallo, Liebchen.* Did you have a *gut* rest?" Faith asked in a soft voice, knowing the girl needed a moment to wake up fully.

"Ja." Adel breathed deeply as she cuddled against her chest.

"I'm glad you're awake. We're going to ride into town and buy some supplies. Would you like that?" Faith asked in a soothing tone as she tidied the girl's hair and smoothed her prayer *kapp.*

That got the child's attention. She nodded and sat up straight. "Ziah come, too?"

Faith released a sigh of resignation, wondering how the child had formed such a quick attachment to the man.

"*Ja*, Josiah needs some supplies as well, so he's going to drive us. We better get ready."

Faith patted the girl's back and set her on her feet. Adel hurried to her room to put on her shoes. Minutes later, they were outside and loaded into the wagon.

As usual, Adel sat between Faith and Josiah. The girl babbled happily as she pretended to feed her doll a cracker. They arrived in town soon enough and Josiah pulled the wagon to a halt in front of the real estate office. While he waited outside with Adel, Faith went inside and met briefly with Vance Anderson, a real estate agent she knew had helped a number of Amish people in the past.

When she stepped outside again, Faith stood on the front steps for several moments, secretly watching Josiah and Adel. Holding the leather leads in her tiny hands, the child sat happily beside the man as she made cute little sounds and pretended to drive the wagon by herself. Twice, Josiah patiently untangled the lines and endured a slap in the face when Adel whipped the leads in the air with a bit too much enthusiasm.

"Careful! Make slow movements," Josiah advised the girl in a patient voice. "Move slow and gentle so you don't spook your horse. Until he knows you well, you want to win his trust so you can work as a team."

"*Ja*, I be more careful, Ziah," Adel told him.

The child lifted the lines cautiously. As she did so, Josiah glanced up and saw Faith standing there.

"Faith!" He immediately jumped down from the wagon and came around to assist her in climbing up.

"How did it go?" he asked as she settled into her seat.

"It went well," she said.

With a nod, he hurried around to the driver's seat. When he was ready, he looked at Adel and spoke most politely.

"Do you mind if I drive now, dilly bean?"

Without hesitation, she handed over the lines. "*Ja*, Ziah. You drive."

Picking up Martha, the child cradled her doll and stared straight ahead, her expression filled with absolute trust.

"Someday, I drive teams of horse. Huh, Ziah?" Adel said, looking at Josiah for approval.

"You sure will, sweetie." With a wide smile, Josiah released the brake and lightly slapped Jack's rump. The giant animal stepped forward and the wagon lurched into motion.

Faith didn't say a word. But in her heart, she thought it was nice that Adel had a good father figure in her life for a change. Back in Ohio, her cousin Sadie had been a widow so there were no men on the farm, except for those they hired to do certain chores. Faith had worried Adel might grow up never knowing what a healthy home life with a mother and father was like.

"Did the Realtor give you the information you hoped for?" Josiah asked her.

Faith nodded. "*Ja*, he said he'd run some numbers and do some comparisons and get back to me with a suggested sell price in a few days or so."

"*Ach*, so you don't know what your asking price for the farm will be yet?"

"Not yet. But I promise to give you the first option to buy the place," she said.

She knew he was eager to find out what she wanted for the farm, so he could determine if he could buy it from her. And honestly, she wanted to sell it to him. He knew her land almost as well as she did and she couldn't think of anyone who would love and care for it more than him. But deep in her heart of hearts, she couldn't imagine not living there herself. She really had no choice, though.

Riding down Main Street, Faith was startled when she saw Mervin and Hannah Schwartz entering the grocery store. In addition to farming, the middle-aged Amish couple had seven children and owned a small sawmill and goat herd. Upon seeing them, the Schwartzes paused and waved.

"Hallo!" Hannah called, waggling her fingers at them.

"Guder daag!" Josiah didn't stop but lifted his hand in greeting.

Pasting a smile on her face, Faith returned their wave and inwardly groaned. She hadn't considered the possibility that she might see other Amish people in town. Now it would be all over their *Gmay* by next church Sunday that she and Josiah were seen out and about together. Everyone in her congregation would assume they were getting back together. And they weren't. But that wouldn't stop the gossip.

Josiah pulled the horse and wagon to a halt behind the feed and grain store. As he helped Faith and Adel down from the contraption, a bit of confusion fogged his brain. Faith insisted she must sell her farm and leave town, yet she wanted to buy chickens for the coop he was repairing. She could easily sell the birds with the farm, once she turned the place over to a buyer. But it almost seemed as if she was warring within herself. She obviously loved her home and wanted to stay. So, why the insistence to sell? It didn't make sense. Not to him.

He held the door for her as they stepped inside the store. Immediately, the pungent scent of seeds and sawdust struck him in the face. Shoppers milled around, perusing the shelves for bags of feed, bedding, farm tools and even a bit of lumber. As the only farm store in town, this place carried it all.

Toward the back wall, baby chickens swarmed around a large pen set up with shallow dishes of water, seeds and electric warming lamps. Pointing out the birds, Josiah pressed the flat of his hand against Faith's lower back to urge her in that direction.

"Why don't you check out the birds? I'll get the boards and wire I need and meet you there in a few minutes," Josiah said.

"Danke." Faith took hold of Adel's hand and led her daughter over to the chicks.

The moment the child saw the fuzzy babies, she let out a squeal of delight, dropped her dolly on the floor and ran toward the enclosure.

Faith scooped up Martha. Smiling at the girl, Josiah went about his business, heading outside into the wide yard where they kept stacks of lumber. He soon had a bale of chicken wire and three pine boards piled into the back of the wagon. When he returned to load Faith's chickens, he stood off and watched her and Adel for several minutes. The girl sat smack-dab in the middle of the enclosure. Fuzzy little chicks swarmed around her, their *peep-peeps* filling the air. The child held one tiny baby in her hands, her face alight with absolute joy. Faith sat nearby on a low bench, holding four of the babies in her lap. She checked each one over carefully, then placed them in a smaller pen to sequester them from the bigger group.

Gazing at her daughter, Faith reached forward from time to time to speak quietly and direct Adel in *Deitsch.* "Be gentle, dilly bean. Remember it's a *boppli.* You don't want to hurt them. They are small and helpless. You must be careful."

Adel nodded and spoke in a reverent whisper as she petted one soft little chick. "*Ja*, I careful, *Mammi*."

Faith lifted one of the tiny birds and brushed its downy softness against Adel's cheek. The child immediately squealed with pleasure, her giggles of delight filling the air.

Both the woman's and child's faces contained utter rapture. Josiah chuckled to himself, wondering how a few squawking birds could seduce almost every woman and child into adoration. Watching the girls interact with the babies, a warm and hazy feeling blanketed Josiah. And for one tumultuous moment, he couldn't help thinking this should have been his *familye*. Resentment swarmed his chest. Why had Faith taken this from them?

Adel caught sight of Josiah and called to him. "Look, Ziah. The *hinkli* tickle me."

"I see," he said, coming to stand nearby.

The moment she saw him watching her, Faith's smile faded. Lurching to her feet, she set the chick she'd been holding aside in the selection pen, then brushed off her skirts. Once more, Josiah wondered why Faith had born a child out of wedlock. She must have loved Adel's father in order to get caught with his babe. The fine property she'd inherited would fill any Amish man with absolute glee. Unless the man was *Englisch*, which Josiah doubted. Yet, Faith was alone. She'd never married and planned to sell the place as soon as possible. Why?

"I'd like to buy those chicks, please." Faith spoke to a salesclerk as she pointed to the smaller pen, which held a dozen of the cutest, fluffiest yellow babies Josiah had ever seen.

"You have a *gut* eye. From the looks of them, you've picked what appears to be the largest, healthiest *hinkli*," he said.

Conscious of several people standing nearby, he spoke in *Deitsch*, knowing the *Englisch* couldn't understand his words.

"*Ja*, I thought they'd reach maturity sooner. I'd love to have fresh eggs on the farm, though I know it'll take some time." She stepped inside the larger pen and picked up another little bird.

"When is Adel's birthday?" he asked.

"March the third." She spoke absentmindedly as she perused the baby.

"Hmm, that would have been eight months after you left town," he said.

She jerked her head up, her eyes filled with shock, and he wondered at her reaction. Before he could question her further, she turned aside, as if she didn't want to talk about it. But now, Josiah felt more confused than ever. Adel's birthdate meant Faith had been expecting a child when she'd left town so suddenly. And since Josiah knew he wasn't the father, that meant Faith had been cheating on him. But that didn't seem right. At the time, Josiah had believed their love was real. She wouldn't have been stepping out on him with someone else. News traveled too fast in this small community. He would have heard about it before now. But maybe someone had taken ill advantage of her. Had someone forced himself on her?

"Adel, we've got to go, sweetie," she said, sliding a chick out of the child's hands.

As she set the bird on the floor, Adel scooped up another one and stubbornly shook her head. "*Ne*, I stay. You go, *Mammi*."

Faith laughed and glanced at him, then over to the cash register, where several *Englisch* people were watching them with open curiosity. Most of the Amish were used to such gawking. With their unique clothing, horses and buggies, they were an oddity most *Englischers* couldn't seem to ignore.

"We can't stay. We've got to go, Adel. Right now." Faith spoke in a stern whisper but the girl was unmoved.

"*Ne*, I stay," Adel said.

The salesclerk handed Josiah a crate made of slender pieces of wood and chicken wire. "You can put the birds your wife wants to buy in this. But there's a five-dollar deposit on the cage. You'll have to return it to the store within a week."

His wife! Josiah's thoughts scattered. Faith wasn't his spouse but he didn't get the chance to explain. A commotion at the front register drew his attention.

Anne Clarke, an *Englisch* woman who lived in the largest house in town, stood several paces behind her husband, Frank. Wearing blue jeans and a short haircut, Anne had salt-and-pepper hair that framed her face. As a person with a mobility impairment, she leaned heavily on a wooden cane. Rumor had it that Frank was abusive and had pushed her down a flight of stairs when they'd first married thirty years earlier. As Josiah recalled, Hope had once dated Brian, the Clarkes' only son.

"Come on! Can't you keep up?" Frank sneered at Anne with impatience. A tall, beefy man in his early sixties, he didn't look happy.

Anne glanced over at the baby chicks with longing, her brown eyes filled with insecurity and a deep-seated sadness. Josiah got the impression she wanted to come over and view the tiny birds, but her husband had other ideas.

"Let's go already," Frank snarled, his voice filled with annoyance.

Anne's shoulders hunched and she bowed her head in submission. From what Josiah could see, she was used to being bossed around and dominated by her overbearing husband. The poor lady.

Josiah looked away. As a pacifist, he'd learned early on not to engage with the *Englisch* any more than absolutely necessary. But Frank Clarke's lack of consideration for his wife's lame leg disturbed Josiah. As the wealthiest rancher in the area, Frank had a nasty reputation for getting whatever he wanted, whenever he wanted it. Since Brian, the Clarkes' only child, had been killed in a DUI two years earlier, Josiah figured the loss was partly responsible for Frank's foul temper, but not all of it. Frank had been rude and mean long before Brian died.

Returning his attention to Faith, Josiah noticed she seemed nervous and jittery as she tried to usher Adel out of the chick pen. The little girl wasn't cooperating. Color flooded Faith's face with embarrassment and her forehead and lips curved into a deep frown. The combination of a disobedient child and *Englischers* gaping at her undoubtedly upset Faith.

Reaching down, she gently tried to extricate Adel from the pen without stepping on a bird.

"*Ne, Mammi.* I stay," Adel cried, a scowl on her face as she held tightly to one baby.

"But we've got to go. And see those *hinkli* over there? Those are ours. We're taking them home with us," Faith coaxed, pointing at the crate where Josiah had placed a dozen little chicks that had been handpicked by her.

Adel's countenance lightened. "Those mine?"

The girl pointed at the birds as they fluttered around inside the cage and *peep-peeped* incessantly.

"*Ja*, those are ours. So, can you please *komm* with me right now?" Faith asked again, her voice filled with pleading.

"*Ja*, we go." Adel promptly released the chick she'd been hugging tightly to her chest and took her mommy's hand as Faith lifted her over the barrier.

They headed toward the front cash register and Josiah lifted the crate of birds, bringing up the rear. Faith looked around the store, her eyes wide and searching, as though she feared what people might think of her and her naughty child. Her cheeks still gleamed a pretty shade of pink and he couldn't blame her for feeling mortified by Adel's disobedience. But after all, the little girl was still quite young. He hoped Faith wouldn't be too hard on her.

While Faith paid for their purchases, Josiah took the cage outside and slid it into the back of the wagon, then covered it with an old quilt to keep the babies warm on the ride home. When the girls joined him, he helped them each climb up onto the seat. As he drove the wagon, Josiah would have questioned Faith more about Adel's birth date. Even with the child sitting between them, she didn't speak English yet and they could have talked freely. But why bother? It didn't matter anymore who the girl's father was. What had happened was in the past. Josiah couldn't turn back time and change the outcome. He couldn't make Faith love him, nor could he love her again. Because learning that she might have cheated on him was a huge reminder that he couldn't trust this woman. Especially not with his heart.

Chapter Seven

Using her hoe, Faith raked the last long, tidy furrow in her garden plot. Since Josiah had tilled the earth for her recently, the ground was soft, slightly damp and extremely malleable. The dirt was completely free of rocks and filled with nutrient-rich mulch. Perfect garden soil.

Early-morning sunlight gleamed across the yard, shining against the large red barn and sheds. She'd been working for over an hour now, deeply lost in her thoughts. Buying baby chicks yesterday hadn't been as much fun as she'd thought. Everything had been fine, until she'd looked up and seen Frank and Anne Clarke standing at the front of the store. Brian's parents were the two other people Faith wanted to avoid at all costs. The moment she'd caught sight of them, she'd tried to act normal…just a plain Amish woman shopping in town with her little girl. But inside, she'd been trembling. Frank had paid them no mind at all, but Anne had stared long and hard, leaning heavily on her cane. Undoubtedly, she recognized Faith. They'd only met once but she was her sister's identical twin.

And garnering Anne's attention was the last thing Faith wanted or needed right now.

Josiah had appeared surprised when Faith insisted they leave immediately. Though he had turned and seen the Clarkes, he hadn't commented on them or the fact that Hope used to date their son. Feeling guilty, Faith hoped he never guessed the connection. The last thing she wanted was to answer his questions about Hope, Adel, and why she'd been gone four long years. But there was no way Josiah could ever know the full truth. Not unless she told him. And she would never do that.

This morning, when Faith saw his buggy pull into the yard just before dawn, she had stepped outside and closed the door quietly so she wouldn't awaken Adel. That had given her time to work without interruption. Now she had no idea where Josiah was. Somewhere on the farm. Possibly out in the fields. Adel would be waking up soon and wanting her breakfast. This was a good stopping point.

Standing straight, Faith arched her spine to relieve the dull ache in her shoulders and lifted her face to catch the cooling breeze. She'd fed the baby chicks before coming outside. The first day of May was lovely and clear but still too chilly for the babies to be housed in the newly repaired chicken coop. Until the fuzzy little birds gained a bit more size and the weather warmed up in a couple more weeks, they'd live in a tall box beside the woodstove in the kitchen. There, it was toasty warm and they could thrive until they were big enough to move outdoors.

Glancing at the garden, Faith nodded with satisfaction at her work. With a quarter of an acre of rich, dark soil, she had plenty of room to grow whatever she liked.

The long furrows she'd shaped were all ready for her to plant a wide variety of seeds and twenty tomato plants. By autumn, she'd have a plethora of vegetables to bottle, including cabbage, beets, turnips, beans and potatoes. Because she planned not to be here for the harvest, she hated the thought of the food going to waste. Before she left town, she'd make arrangements for the women in her *Gmay* to come and pick what she grew.

Heaving a deep sigh, she stepped over the furrows of freshly turned dirt toward the house. It would take all day to plant and water everything. Before she continued her work, she should check on Adel.

As she passed the barn, she caught the distinct sound of the little girl's sweet laughter coming from the corrals. When had the child come outside?

Veering off in that direction, Faith stepped up on the bottom rung of the rail fence and peered over the top. When Jack, one of Josiah's big Percheron draft horses, pranced into view, Faith lost her grip and almost fell off the fence. Clutching for the wooden post, she stared as the big horse lifted his giant head and swung around in a wide arc. Something had startled the animal as he picked up his long legs and strutted around the perimeter of the enclosure. The stallion seemed playful and full of life this morning. At that moment, Adel raced past the barn door, squealing with merriment.

"Adel!" Faith cried.

The child didn't seem to hear as she ran back into the barn. Realizing her child was scurrying around the barnyard beneath the hooves of giant horses, a blaze of panic dotted Faith's skin. The girl might be trampled!

In a flurry of movement, Faith ducked beneath a rail and scrambled over the fence into the paddock. Hurrying past Jack, she sprinted toward the barn…and came to a halt just beyond the wide double doors. Tilly stood against one side of the fence, her left back leg lifted so the front tip of her hoof rested lightly against the ground. The mare stood perfectly still and watched with calm indifference as Adel scampered past, giggling her head off.

"You not catch me, Ziah. I too fast," Adel yelled over her shoulder.

Josiah ran into view, lifting a hand as he pursued the girl in a game of chase. His rumbling chuckle filled the air as he dodged this way and that, seeming to purposefully let the child evade his reach.

"*Ach*, I will catch you, dilly bean. I'm fast, too," he called, his fingertips brushing against her arm without taking hold.

He ducked beneath the tall mare's muzzle. Tilly didn't blink or budge. In fact, the horse looked completely bored with the situation and Faith was beyond grateful the mare was so calm and well-trained.

The sound of Josiah's low chortle triggered a poignant spark deep inside Faith, a feeling she thought was long dead. She'd always loved Josiah's laugh. It was masculine, unique and so genuine. But why was he playing with Adel around the large horses? The child could be hurt!

"Adel! Stop!" Faith called loud and clear.

Josiah came to a sudden halt, looking at her, his mouth hanging open in surprise.

"Faith! I didn't know you were here," he said.

Adel paused just beside Tilly's right front leg. The girl had obviously dressed herself that morning. Her apron was askew and tufts of her golden curls framed her face from beneath her crooked prayer *kapp.*

Wrapping one little arm around the gray horse's leg, the child stood on top of Tilly's plate-sized hoof and leaned casually against the mare's forearm. Still the horse didn't move, solid as a rock. Compared to the animal's huge hoof, Adel's teeny feet looked so diminutive. And that's when Faith noticed something very odd about Adel's shoes.

Realizing the problem, Faith swallowed a giggle. If she hadn't been so frightened for her child, she would have snickered out loud. Her face must have betrayed her mirth because Josiah tilted his head in bewilderment, then looked down at the girl's feet…and promptly burst into laughter. Adel had put her shoes on the wrong feet. Her plain black Mary Janes were turning out where they should have turned in. With little room for her toes, the shoes were undoubtedly pinching Adel's feet, yet the girl didn't seem to notice.

"Sweetie, are your shoes uncomfortable this morning?" Josiah asked, his handsome mouth twitching in a concealed grin.

Adel glanced down in confusion, then shook her head. "*Ne.* They fine, Ziah. Why?"

Jack stepped near and nudged Tilly's rump with his nose. In response, the mare gingerly stepped forward, as if she knew the child was there and needed to be protected. Adel hopped off the horse's hoof and darted beneath the mare's underbelly as the horses headed inside the barn for their breakfast. Adel was forced to hurry out of the way or be trampled.

"That's it! Adel, we're going to the house," Faith said, scooping the child into her arms.

"*Ne!* I stay with Ziah," Adel cried.

"*Ne*, it's not safe for a small *kind* to be running around beneath these big horses," Faith said.

"I not running. I skipping," Adel argued, her impudent nose crinkled in a frown.

"It doesn't matter. You shouldn't be around the draft horses," Faith said.

Josiah stepped forward. "That's my fault, Faith. We were just playing. But I know my horses. Adel was never in any real danger."

A vision of Adel being trampled filled Faith's mind. Remembering her poor, dead sister and the promise she'd made to keep Adel safe, Faith felt a tremble of fear wash over her. Standing beside the gate, she struggled to keep her hold on Adel as the girl squirmed to get free.

"Let go, *Mammi*. Let go!"

"You should know better, Josiah. Adel is only three years old. She's way too small to be running free beneath the bellies of your big horses. I can't believe you were so careless," she scolded.

Josiah blinked in astonishment and opened his mouth as if he wanted to speak, but then remained silent.

"*Mammi*, I play," Adel cried, pushing against Faith's shoulders with the palms of her hands.

"You can play inside the house after you've had your breakfast," Faith said.

Brushing past the Percherons, Faith hurried through the barn toward the main doors. She ignored Josiah's startled expression until she was outside in the backyard. As she headed toward the house, she noticed a blue car parked along the county road about a quarter of a mile away. A woman dressed in *Englisch* clothes

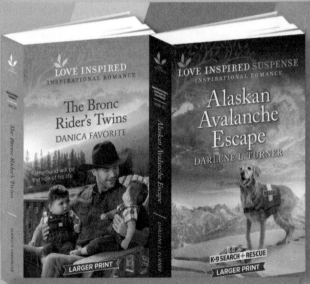

Get Free Books In Just 3 Easy Steps

Are you an avid reader searching for more books?
The **Harlequin Reader Service** might be for you! We'd love to send you up to **4 free books** just for trying it out. Just write **"YES"** on the **Free Books Voucher Card** and we'll send your free books and a gift, altogether worth over $20.

Step 1: Choose your Books

Try *Love Inspired® Romance Larger-Print* and get 2 books and fall in love with inspirational romances that take you on an uplifting journey of faith, forgiveness and hope.

Try *Love Inspired® Suspense Larger-Print* and get 2 books where courage and optimism unite in stories of faith and love in the face of danger.

Or *TRY BOTH!*

Step 2: Return your completed Free Books Voucher Card

Step 3: Receive your books and continue reading!

Your free books are **completely free**, even the shipping! If you continue with your subscription, you can look forward to curated monthly shipments of brand-new books from your selected series, always at a discount off the cover price! Plus you can cancel any time.

Don't miss out, reply today! Over $20 FREE value.

Free Books Voucher Card

was staring straight at the farm with what appeared to be a pair of binoculars. From this distance, Faith couldn't make out the identity of the stranger. Maybe they were a potential buyer interested in purchasing the farm.

"*Mammi*, let go. I play with Ziah," Adel cried as Faith carried her to the house.

"Not right now. You need to eat first," Faith insisted.

As she threw open the screen door and deposited Adel on the floor inside the kitchen, Faith had to distract the child with the baby chicks. Once she got Adel strapped into her wooden high chair and she was eating freshly scrambled eggs and bacon, the girl settled down and they returned to their normal routine. But thirty minutes later, Faith insisted Adel help her plant carrot seeds in the garden to keep the child from running back to the corrals. The blue car up on the county road was long gone.

Shortly afterward, Faith saw Josiah take his big draft horses out to the hayfields and she relaxed. But even then, she kept a close watch over Adel as they labored in the garden, in case the child decided to follow him.

Faith couldn't understand the close attachment Adel had with Josiah. He wasn't the girl's father. He was nothing to them but a member of their *Gmay*. And yet, the child wanted to be with him all the time. That wasn't safe. They were leaving town soon. Faith didn't want Adel to form a powerful attachment that would upset the girl when they sold the farm and left. But more than that, Josiah was a smart man. Sometimes, Faith saw him watching Adel with an astute look that told her he was thinking hard about the child. What if he guessed the truth? If he knew her secret, would he keep it or reveal it to others? Faith no longer knew the man she used to love. Could she trust him to keep her secret?

No! She couldn't take the chance. In the future, it would be best if she and Adel kept their distance from Josiah.

Josiah worked late that evening. The sun was close to setting when he finally returned his Percherons to the barn, rubbed them down good, and ensured they had plenty of food and water. As was his routine, he fed Billy and Bean, too. As he watched Billy munch his hay, Josiah shook his head. He still couldn't understand Faith's sentimentality in keeping the ancient horse. But having a friend seemed good for Bean, who got along well with the old gelding.

Satisfied that all was well for the night, he harnessed his road horse to his buggy and pulled them over to the side of Faith's farmhouse. She'd been mighty upset early that morning when he'd been playing chase in the corrals with Adel. For some reason, he wanted to apologize and reassure Faith.

Stepping up onto the back deck, he knocked lightly on the screen door. It was rather late and he didn't want to awaken Adel if she was already asleep.

A single gaslight gleamed from the ceiling in the kitchen. A sound from the front of the house told him Faith had heard his knock. As he waited for her to come to the door, he peered at the pristine table, sink and countertops. He already noticed she'd planted an enormous garden, too. Faith had always been an orderly, organized person with a strong work ethic. But if she truly wanted to leave town, what was she going to do with all those vegetables once harvest season arrived?

She appeared in the doorway leading to the living room. Peering at the door, she looked worried until she recognized him. Wearing a modest bathrobe, she padded across the shiny floor in bare feet. Her prayer *kapp* was slightly askew and long tendrils of golden hair framed her face. From her disheveled appearance, he thought she must have been preparing for bed and hastily pulled her hair up and covered it with the *kapp* before answering his call.

"Josiah!" she said, her beautiful blue eyes wide and filled with doubt.

Pushing the screen door open, she stepped outside before closing it softly behind her. Then, she folded her arms as she met his gaze.

"It's late. I thought you had already left for the day. Why are you still here?" She spoke quietly, her expression filled with apprehension.

"We'll lose the irrigation water at midnight and I wanted to ensure the orchard and fields had a *gut* soaking before I left for the day," he said.

She nodded in understanding. The local farmers shared the water and took their assigned turns drawing off of the ditch. In a pinch, they could siphon water from the creek running through their farm, but that would deplete it rapidly and they might need it later, toward the end of summer. "*Danke.* I appreciate you being so conscientious. But you really should go *heemet* now. It's not safe to drive your horse and buggy in the dark. The cars and trucks whizz along the roads way too fast and I don't want you involved in an accident."

Her praise and worry touched his heart. But her stiff

shoulders and pursed lips told him she was irritated by him. And he thought he knew why.

"I just wanted to say I'm sorry about what happened earlier in the corrals today. I didn't mean any harm," he said.

She ducked her head, no longer meeting his eyes. "*Danke* for the apology. It was rather careless of you. I'd rather Adel not be running around the barnyard with the livestock."

Her words of chastisement bit hard into his heart and he felt a fissure of tension settle in his spine. After all, Faith was Adel's mother and should have been keeping a better eye on the child.

"You're right. When she came out to the barn alone, I endeavored to look after her. I didn't know where you were," he said, trying hard not to find fault.

Faith's cheeks flushed a pretty shade of pink and she had the good grace to look embarrassed. She nodded. "You're right. I should have checked on her sooner. I was planting the garden and getting so much work done, I lost track of time. I thought Adel was still asleep and I'm not sure how she snuck out of the house without me seeing her. I'm sorry."

With her apology, he thought the matter was settled and they could put it behind them. But her tight lips and unyielding frown told him differently.

"My horses are gentle giants and I was always close by, watching over Adel. She really needs to get used to working around farm animals. There's no need for us to overreact about this," he said.

He meant well but her eyes narrowed. Though she didn't speak for several moments, he thought she must be steaming inside.

Reaching for the door, she opened it and stepped back inside. When she turned, she spoke through the screen and he felt that barrier between them like a brick wall.

"*Danke* again. Have a safe journey *heemet*," she said, her expression stoic and her words clipped.

He stood there, at a loss for something more to say, as she closed the solid door and flipped the dead bolt. And still he didn't move as she turned off the gaslight and left the kitchen.

Moments later, he stepped over to his buggy and climbed inside. As he released the parking brake and gathered the leather lines in his hands, he glanced up and saw her silhouette in her bedroom window on the second floor. The light went out upstairs and he thought she must be going to sleep now.

After he slapped the leads against his horse's rump, the animal stepped forward. The buggy bounced lightly over the graveled driveway as they headed toward the county road.

Feeling out of sorts, Josiah thought over the conversation they'd just had. Though they'd both apologized and she'd thanked him for being diligent in watering her farm, he couldn't help thinking she was peeved with him. And he didn't know why. Little Adel had never been in any real danger with his horses. Not with him standing so close by. In fact, Josiah liked how at ease she was with the animals. As an Amish girl, Adel would grow up around lots of livestock. It was best for her not to fear them.

He never thought Faith was frightened of draft horses, either. As he searched his memory, he couldn't remember a single time in their childhood when she'd been skittish around any of the multitude of horses, cattle, goats and pigs they'd each had on their farms. So, what was the reason for her overreaction to Adel playing in the corrals with him today?

Shaking his head, he couldn't figure it out. He loved Adel very much. She was a sweet, guileless little girl. In fact, she reminded Josiah of Faith when she'd been young. But he had to remember that they were leaving soon. All the work Josiah was doing on this farm was purely to get it ready to sell to an interested buyer. And in his heart of hearts, he hoped that would be him.

In a short time, Faith would return to town and meet with the Realtor again. Soon, she'd know how much her farm was worth. She'd promised to give him the first option. And once he knew her asking price, they could sit down together and determine if he could buy the place. After that, Faith and Adel would leave town and he wouldn't see them anymore. It was what Faith wanted. And if that was so, Josiah tried to be happy for her. And yet, he felt as though he was losing his best friend. Again. Which didn't make sense. Because he'd lost Faith long ago. Four years, to be exact. And the sooner he accepted that she was leaving and not coming back, the better. He would have a fine farm of his own and would marry someone from his *Gmay.* Soon, he'd have a *familye* of his own to love. Everything was going great for him. He couldn't be happier.

So, why did he feel so rotten inside?

Chapter Eight

As the days passed, Faith made a conscious effort to avoid Josiah as much as possible. She feared Adel was way too fond of the attractive Amish man. Maybe Faith was becoming overly attached to him, too.

She and Adel attended church again and it was much easier this time. No one asked intrusive questions. It was almost as if she'd never left. Like before, they sat on the back row. Josiah watched them quietly from across the room but stayed away during lunch. Maybe he wanted to put distance between them, too.

As promised, Adel played with the other children and had a blast. After the service, several men asked Faith details about how much acreage she had, but no one seemed genuinely interested in buying her place. They were just curious. After all, most of them already owned their own farms. Like a sentinel, the bishop's wife stayed nearby and none of the other women asked pointed questions about Hope's death or Adel's father. They seemed to have accepted her back into the fold, though old Marva Geingerich still gazed at Faith with a heavy, disapproving glower. Trina Graber did likewise, though the girl's expression seemed more sad and disappointed than anything else.

Late the following week, Faith took Adel outside. She had no idea where Josiah was but knew he must be around somewhere. Out in the pasture, knee-high grass shivered in the mild morning breeze. Jack and Tilly grazed peacefully alongside Billy and Josiah's road horse. It was the second week in May and a bright, warm sun gleamed across the yard as she headed toward the barn with Adel in tow. Apparently Josiah wasn't using his big draft horses today. Hoping to avoid him altogether, Faith stepped inside the dim interior of the barn and set her purse on a bale of hay before lifting Adel to sit on a low stool.

"Where we go, *Mammi*?" Adel asked, cradling Martha in her lap.

"I need to speak to the Realtor in town again and buy a few groceries. We don't need much. Just a few things." Faith spoke as she led the new road horse out of his stall.

"*Hallo*, Bean!" Adel called, waving as if the horse understood her every word.

When the child tried to slide off the stool, Faith shook her head. "*Ne*, Adel. You stay right there until I'm finished, sweetums. I don't want Bean to trample you."

As expected, the child obeyed. "He not trample me, *Mammi*. Bean lubs me."

"Of course he does. I love you, too," Faith said as she backed the horse into position in front of the buggy.

The gelding didn't fight her one bit, his manner easy and mild. Josiah had trained him well and Faith couldn't help feeling impressed by the man's skill with horses.

"Where Ziah?" Adel asked, glancing at the empty animal stalls.

Taking a deep inhale, Faith shrugged but didn't look up from her task. "I have no idea. I'm sure he's working here someplace."

The air smelled of fresh, clean straw. Josiah had swept each cubicle spotless so they were ready for livestock once the new owner bought the place. He did everything with immaculate precision. No doubt, he would make some woman a fine Amish husband.

"I find Ziah."

Before Faith could stop her, Adel slid off the stool and hurried toward the back doors, her little black shoes clicking against the wooden floor.

"Adel, *komm* back here. Josiah is busy and I don't want you bothering him," Faith called, her voice slightly stern.

In truth, she didn't want him to tag along. Being in his presence was a glaring reminder of what they'd once shared and how both their hearts had been broken. It was best to stay away from him, if possible.

"Ahh," Adel grouched, her sweet face creased in a frown. But she obediently returned and plopped Martha onto the stool in a disgruntled flop.

"*Hallo* there! Did I hear someone call my name?"

Faith snapped around as the very man she was trying to avoid strode confidently into the barn carrying a heavy hammer and a clear, empty compartment box for nails.

"Ziah!" Adel cried, racing toward him.

Great! So much for sneaking off into town without meeting up with him first.

As the child scurried past, Bean jerked his head up

and pranced nervously to one side. Thankfully, Faith
already had him harnessed to the buggy. Lifting her
hand, she sought to steady the agitated horse. Though
he was well-trained, he was still young and probably
not used to little kids running past him.

Josiah placed his tools on the workbench, then
reached to pick up Adel in a swinging arc that made
her giggle. In the process, the child dropped Martha to
the ground and barely spared the doll a second glance.

"Hi there, dilly bean!" Josiah said.

With his movements, his straw hat was knocked to
the floor. His chestnut hair was slightly tousled and his
dark eyes sparkled with a wide smile. Wearing a dark
blue collarless shirt, Josiah looked rugged and more
handsome than a man had a right to be.

As he held the girl with one arm, he reached out and
smoothed his free hand against Bean's neck to calm
the restless animal.

"There, boy. Stand!" he commanded.

The horse immediately settled, his ears pricked forward with attention. Taking hold of Adel's fingers with
his, Josiah showed the tiny girl how to run her palm
over the animal's neck and taught her what to say.

"There, Bean. It's *allrecht*. Stand!" Adel said.

Faith stared at the two in wonder. It was as if they
were kindred spirits. In that simple action, Josiah had
just started teaching the girl how to train a horse. This
was Hope's child. They'd only been here a handful of
weeks, yet Josiah had already become more of a father
to Adel than any man alive.

Faith looked away, feeling bewildered as she lifted
the leather lead lines into place within the buggy.

"Where are you going?" Josiah asked with a smile.

"To town. *Mammi* not need much," Adel said.

Josiah laughed, the sound deep and rumbling like thunder off in the distance. Faith ignored her child's happy chatter as she told him exactly what they were planning to do.

Josiah glanced at Faith. "This is perfect timing. I've been repairing the pig pen and also need a few things to finish my work. Mind if I drive you there?"

Hmm. She didn't think it was perfect timing.

"I could pick the items up for you while I'm there," she offered.

He pursed his lips. "It's better if I do it myself. And the bishop did ask me to look after you two."

Yeah, the bishop again. What could she say without sounding rude? She tossed a dubious glance at the buggy.

"Will we need to change over to the wagon again?" she asked.

He set Adel on her feet and patted the child's soft cheek. Adel beamed with delight.

"*Ne*, I think the buggy is big enough for today," he said. "I just need some more nails, clips and several ground stakes. They should fit just fine on the floor of the back seat."

Adel scooped up Martha from the ground, brushed the dirt off the doll's skirt, then hurried over to the buggy.

"Let's go, Ziah!" She spoke happily, trying to climb inside by herself.

While Josiah checked the harness and nodded his approval, Faith retrieved her purse. She lifted Adel into the buggy, then strapped the girl into her child safety seat.

"*Danke, Mammi.* I lub you," the girl said.

Gazing at her child's sweet face, Faith's heart gave a powerful squeeze. "Oh, how I love you too, sweetums."

Josiah cleared his throat nearby and Faith hurriedly sat on the seat and closed the buggy door. Within moments, Josiah joined them and off they went. Like a normal *familye* driving into town to do a little shopping. Except they weren't. And they never would be.

"Why don't I drop you off at the Realtor's office while I head over to the feed and grain? Then, I can meet you over at the general store," Josiah said.

Separating while they ran their errands suited Faith just fine. "*Ja*, that sounds like a plan."

"*Ach*, I shouldn't be long. I can carry your groceries for you," he said.

"*Mammi* not need much," Adel chimed in.

Faith almost laughed. Nothing escaped this alert little girl's notice. She was way too smart for her own good.

They arrived at the real estate office in record speed and Josiah helped them out of the buggy. Faith barely spared him a glance as he bid them farewell.

Twenty minutes later, she was holding Adel's hand as they walked along the boardwalk toward the general store. After what she'd just learned from the Realtor, she felt like she was floating on seafoam. Never in her wildest dreams would she have believed her aunt and uncle's farm was worth so much. To her, it was a huge, exorbitant amount. What if Josiah couldn't afford the high price? It was way more money than Faith had ever imagined. The Amish lived rather frugally, growing most of what they ate and sewing most of their clothes. If Josiah couldn't pay the price, she would sell the place to him for the amount she needed to purchase a modest home in Ohio. Coupled with the savings Aunt Fern had left her at the bank, that should be sufficient for her and Adel's needs. To earn extra cash, Faith could work on her cousin's farm or as a waitress in the local Amish diner. It wasn't the loving husband and *familye* Faith had dreamed of having but at least she could raise Adel in comfort and peace.

Inside the general store, she lifted Adel into the child seat of her shopping cart and wheeled her down the aisles as she picked several items off the shelves. On a lark, she decided to celebrate her good news by buying Adel an ice-cream bar.

After completing her shopping, Faith took Adel over to the freezer case. It took five minutes for the child to choose which treat she wanted. The salesclerk smiled as Faith unwrapped the bar and handed it to the girl. A movement by the front door caught Faith's eye and she glanced that way. Then, she inwardly groaned. Anne Clarke stood there watching them closely. To make matters worse, Josiah rounded the corner into the store at that exact moment.

Seeing Anne, a rush of panic clawed Faith's throat but she held perfectly still. Preoccupied by her ice cream, Adel didn't notice. Anne took a wobbly step toward them on her cane. And just like that, Faith felt as though her heart dropped out of her chest. She couldn't breathe. Couldn't move. This was one of the critical moments she'd been dreading ever since she'd arrived in town weeks earlier.

She'd had to face Josiah and her Amish congregation. But how could she face Anne Clarke? This was her child's biological grandmother! The biggest threat to her happiness.

"Faith, is that you?" Anne said, her voice gentle and kind.

Faith cleared her throat and clasped the shopping cart handle with whitened knuckles to keep her hands from shaking.

"Um, yes, it's me," she said, speaking perfect English.

"You look just like Hope. I can't get over the resemblance. It's so uncanny. You two look exactly alike," Anne said, standing right beside her.

Adel sat perfectly still, watching the stranger as she licked her ice cream. She stared with her wide, beautiful blue eyes.

"Is this your daughter?" Anne asked, smiling at Adel.

That did it. Faith's courage almost failed her. She felt as though the blood had drained from her face.

Stepping around the cart, she placed herself between her child and the *Englisch* woman. It was a protective gesture Faith couldn't resist. She fought against the urge to forget her groceries, snatch Adel from the cart and race out of the store. It took every bit of willpower she could muster to get a grip on her nerves and control her facial expressions. Because no matter what happened next, no one must ever suspect the truth. She must not do anything to reveal her secret. Not to Anne and not to Josiah, who stood near the cash register, watching this exchange with avid interest.

Something was wrong with Faith. Josiah sensed it with every fiber of his being. Though she seemed calm and collected, her face looked white as a sheet and void of expression. He knew this woman so well. The slight tensing of her shoulders. The way she held her head just a bit higher. The subtle widening of her eyes, and the tight grip she had on her shopping cart.

Faith was upset and he couldn't blame her. Everyone in town knew Hope and Brian Clarke had been dating. Most people also knew Brian had always had a foul temper, just like his father. Because Josiah had been close to Faith at one time, he also knew Brian had hit Hope on several occasions. Josiah had been over at her house when he'd heard her aunt Fern talking about it. Both the elderly woman and Faith had pleaded with Hope to stop seeing the *Englisch* man. And for that reason alone, Josiah believed Faith's reaction to Brian's mother was perfectly natural.

"Hope always had such a calming influence on my Brian. I so wish they could have married. But I heard Hope died a few years ago. I'm so sorry for your loss," Anne said, her words sounding sincere.

Faith didn't speak but she nodded, her stilted smile not reaching her eyes. From past conversations they'd had, Josiah knew she never wanted Hope to marry Brian Clarke. Not in a million years.

"It must have been difficult for you to lose your identical twin sister so young," Anne continued, her voice full of compassion.

Faith nodded, her expression strained as she swallowed hard. "Yes, it was."

"But now, you've got this sweet little girl to love." Anne smiled and reached out to gently caress Adel's arm.

As if she was shy of strangers, the child leaned against her mommy and ducked her head, peering at the *Englisch* lady in a sidelong gaze.

Josiah had only met Anne Clarke on a few rare occasions. Each time, she had been soft-spoken, polite and retiring. In fact, the woman seemed the complete opposite of her domineering husband. Frank Clarke was loud, demanding and rude. And Brian, his son, had been exactly like him. Josiah had avoided the Clarkes whenever possible. When Brian had been killed a couple of years earlier in a DUI, Josiah knew of no one, *Englisch* or Amish, who missed him much.

Except perhaps his brokenhearted mother.

"I was wondering, why did Hope leave town so suddenly? How did she die?" Anne asked. Her face was filled with an earnest desire to know, her damp eyes shimmering with genuine grief.

"I...I'm sorry, but I really must get back home as soon as possible. I...I have bread dough rising that needs to be put into the oven to bake," Faith said.

Moving past the woman, Faith wheeled her cart over to the front register and swiftly laid her groceries on the conveyer belt. Adel sat in her seat, her frozen dessert dripping down her little hands.

"Finish your ice cream," Faith said in *Deitsch*.

Adel licked the cone several times before taking a big bite.

Anne followed them, limping slowly on her cane. She stood there watching them, her face filled with doubts and questions she obviously longed to ask.

Josiah couldn't blame Faith for not wanting to talk about her sister in the middle of the grocery store. Especially not with an *Englisch* woman. The Amish kept to themselves whenever possible. Besides that, the twins had always been close. Faith's reticence to chat about her sister's death was completely understandable.

A clerk bagged up Faith's butter, milk, eggs and produce. While Josiah picked up her brown paper bags, Faith snapped open her purse, paid the bill, then lifted Adel out of the cart. Holding tightly to the child's hand, she made a beeline for the door and headed outside toward her horse and buggy. Her stride was stiff and unyielding…and filled with determination.

Anne watched them leave, her face filled with disappointment. For a moment, Josiah felt sorry for the woman. Even if she had wanted to hurry after Faith, she couldn't do so on her lame leg. Though Hope had dated Anne's son, Josiah never realized the woman had been so attached to Hope.

Josiah stashed the shopping bags in the back of the buggy. By the time he came to assist her, Faith had already strapped Adel into her child safety seat and closed the door.

Wow! She really was in a hurry to get home.

As he climbed into the driver's seat and took the lines into his hands, he glanced at Faith. Reaching into her purse, she pulled out a wet wipe and cleaned drips of ice cream off Adel's face and fingers.

"Are you *allrecht*?" he asked, wondering at her abrupt manner.

She glanced his way and flashed an uncertain smile. "*Ja*, I'm fine. Can we go *heemet* now? Please?"

She faced forward, her spine ramrod straight as she stared out the windshield. By all appearances, she looked okay. But something seemed off. Something he couldn't quite put his finger on.

"*Mammi*, who that *fraa*?" Adel asked, pointing out the window.

Anne had stepped outside and was limping heavily

as she made her way tediously down the boardwalk. From the relief etching the corner of Faith's eyes, he could tell she was glad Anne was headed in the opposite direction.

"Just someone I used to know. She's an *Englischer* and we don't mingle with the *Englisch*," Faith said.

Okay, her response sounded logical. It was something all the Amish taught their children. At her young age, Adel didn't need to know more than that. But as Josiah released the parking brake, he wondered why Faith didn't seem to like Anne. The woman was completely different from her husband and always acted so nice.

Adel wasn't satisfied by her mommy's answer, either.

"Why we not like her?" the girl asked.

Faith jerked her head around, looking surprised. "We like her just fine. She's a nice woman. But we're Amish and she's *Englisch*. We have our ways and she has hers. Except to do business, we don't mix with the *Englisch*. Not ever. Do you understand?"

She was looking at her daughter with a strict gaze that demanded obedience.

"Ja," Adel acquiesced, her small voice soft but her eyes filled with more questions.

As they drove home in silence, Josiah couldn't find fault with Faith's explanation. After all, the Amish believed the *Englisch* were too worldly for them to mingle with. For an Amish girl like Hope to be dating an *Englisch* boy like Brian, it had caused a lot of contention and concern for Faith's *familye* and their entire congregation.

Unless they planned to leave their religious beliefs,

an Amish person would never consider walking out with and marrying outside their faith. Hope had constantly crossed the line, leaning toward the *Englisch* world. In time, Josiah feared it would have led to nothing but grief and shunning. Now it was best to raise Adel knowing how they felt about the *Englisch* right from the start.

They didn't speak at all during the ride home and Josiah found himself filled with questions, too. For one thing, he too would like to know how Hope had died. What had taken her life so young? Was it an accident or illness? And why wasn't Adel's father here, caring for his *familye*? How could he ever let go of a woman as beautiful as Faith and her lovely daughter?

For another thing, Josiah was dying to ask Faith what the Realtor had said about her property. What was the value of her farm and how much did she want to sell it to him? But now was not the time to ask. Maybe later, when Adel wasn't around and Faith seemed more like herself.

Undoubtedly, she was still upset by her sister's association with Brian and his *Englisch* parents…especially considering Brian had been known to knock Hope around from time to time. But as they arrived back at Faith's farm and Josiah helped her get Adel and their groceries safely inside the kitchen, he couldn't help glancing over at the tidy counter.

Sitting right there was a large green plastic bowl, covered by a thin white cloth. A large bump was rising up from the middle of the container, suspending the cloth slightly. The room was filled with a pleasant, yeasty aroma. Josiah knew this scene so well. It was the same whenever his mother made bread. She left a large bowl on the counter, covered by a clean cloth, to let the dough rise before she pounded it down to put into greased pans and slide it into the warm oven for baking.

At least Faith had told Anne Clarke the truth. She really did have bread dough rising.

"Do you need me for anything else?" he asked, standing by the back door.

Faith looked up from her chore of putting groceries inside the gas-powered fridge. "*Ne, danke* for your help today."

Her slight frown of irritation belied her kind words.

"You're *willkomm*. I'll be working out in the barnyard if you need me." With a nod, he pushed open the door and stepped outside but held the screen open for several moments.

"Bye, Ziah." Adel waved at him, her face alight with that gorgeous smile she always wore.

A smile so very much like her mother's.

"*Guder daag,*" he returned.

He let the screen clap closed behind him. As he took the horse and buggy to the barn, he couldn't help mulling over what had transpired in town. Maybe he was reading more into the situation than he ought to.

Faith must have been brokenhearted when Hope died. It was logical that she'd be a bit touchy about the subject and not want to discuss it with Anne Clarke. And yet, Josiah sensed there was something more going on here that he couldn't understand. Whatever it was, he doubted Faith would explain it to him. Since her return, there had been a tall cement wall between them. He was her hired hand and nothing more.

Well, that suited him just fine. Because he never wanted to get close to Faith Mast again. His heart couldn't take being broken by her a second time. She would hopefully sell her farm to him and leave town very soon. And that would be that.

So, why did he still have such a bad feeling about it deep down in the pit of his stomach?

Chapter Nine

Faith tilted the heavy water can over a tomato plant and paused as the rush of liquid soaked into the dried earth. When she was satisfied the dirt was saturated so the roots would receive enough moisture, she stood up straight and arched her aching back. Standing at one end of her garden plot, she glanced down the row where Josiah was using another sprinkling pot to douse each plant. As they progressed, they would soon meet in the middle.

Wiping her brow with the back of her arm, she squinted at the early-afternoon sun. The weather had been unseasonably warm. Here in Colorado, they were perpetually in a drought. Hand watering the garden was time-consuming and backbreaking work, but it conserved the precious liquid and allowed her garden to thrive until they received their irrigation water again in a few days.

Glancing at the orchard and barley fields, she hoped they had enough water through the hot summer for her crops to do well. She hoped for a bountiful harvest in the fall…

Wait. For a moment, she'd forgotten she wouldn't be here then, and the thought of leaving made her stare.

"You doing okay?"

She whirled around and found Josiah standing behind her. When she'd started this chore just after lunch, she hadn't expected him to help. But he hadn't even asked before he picked up a pot and started at the opposite end of the row.

"*Ja*, I'm fine. It's a hot one today," she said, grateful Adel was down for her afternoon nap.

"We're almost done. Then, I think I'll check the orchard," he said.

"I don't know how we can ever hand water the fruit trees," she said.

He shrugged and pushed his straw hat back on his head as he looked that way. His dark eyes narrowed in thought. "If I have to, I'll load some barrels in the wagon and haul them out to the orchard and water each tree individually. I can do the same for the hayfield but we might lose the barley. The season is early yet. We won't run out of water until July or August. Let's wait and pray for another *gut* rainstorm before we start worrying."

His words brought her a modicum of comfort. No doubt his father had the same problem over at his farm. But the way Josiah was helping her went above and beyond the call of duty. It was as if they were partners. And they weren't. But since he wanted to buy the place, he had a vested interest in the harvest this autumn.

"Do you think…?" She was interrupted by the sound of an engine.

Swiveling on her heel, she watched a brand-new

black pickup pull into her yard. With one glance, she recognized the man and woman sitting in the front seat.

Oh, no! It felt like Faith's heart had plummeted down to her toes. Frank and Anne Clarke! What were they doing there?

A blaze of panic rushed over Faith. After what happened in town yesterday, she feared Anne might have guessed her secret. But surely that was impossible. She couldn't know the truth. Could she?

"Do you know what they're doing here?" Josiah asked, speaking in *Deitsch*.

"*Ne*, I have no idea." Shaking her head, she set the watering can aside and pulled off her garden gloves.

Anne was Brian's mother. Because Faith considered Brian partly responsible for Hope's death, it was difficult to hide her animosity toward the Clarkes. And that wasn't fair. Anne had never been anything but kind to Hope. In fact, Faith's sister had told her that Brian was often rude to his own mother. The poor woman. If nothing else, she'd deserved her son's and husband's respect. But why were they here now?

Forcing herself to remain calm, Faith stepped over the rows where green plants burgeoned with new life. Brushing at her long skirt, she went to meet the Clarkes.

Frank hopped out of the truck first but didn't go around to help his wife.

Without fanfare, Frank gestured toward the house and farm with a flamboyant sweep of his arm. "You've got a nice place here. I understand you're selling it. Whatever your price, I'd like to buy it."

Faith dropped her mouth open in surprise. Peering at Anne, she watched as the woman held tight to the truck while she lowered herself onto her lame leg. Josiah rushed to help her, clasping the woman's arm until she seemed steady on her feet.

Anne said something to him, but Faith couldn't hear their exchange. She stared at them as he reached inside the truck and pulled out Anne's walking cane, which he handed to her. As the two came to join Frank and Faith, she felt a tap on her shoulder.

"I said, I'd like to buy your farm." Frank glared at her, lifting his beefy hands to rest against his hips.

Blinking at his rudeness, she turned to face the obnoxious man. She gazed at his creased black jeans, shiny Western boots, blue shirt and huge, sparkly belt buckle. By Amish standards, he was full of the world. Towering over her, he exuded power and authority. His jaw was locked hard as granite and she could tell he expected her to give him what he wanted, no questions asked. But the way he treated his wife bit into Faith's heart. Right then and there, something hardened inside of her as she made her final decision. No matter what, this man would never, ever own her farm. Not as long as she had breath in her body.

Conscious of Anne and Josiah standing close within earshot, she lifted her chin an inch higher and met Frank's demanding gaze without flinching.

"I'm sorry, sir. But I've already accepted another offer from someone else. The place is no longer available," she said.

Josiah shifted his weight nervously, his eyes wide with disbelief. He opened his mouth several times to speak but remained silent.

Frank took a step closer, his eyes narrowed. "You've sold it already? Have you signed the final papers?"

She blinked, unwilling to speak a lie. "No, but we will soon."

"Then, it's not a done deal yet. Whatever the price, I'll pay twenty percent more," Frank said.

Twenty percent? That amount seemed unreal. But money wasn't everything. Not to Faith.

"I'm sorry, but I've already given my word. It's finished," she insisted.

"I'll pay double the price," Frank roared.

Wow! This man really did think money could buy anything.

Faith shook her head. "No. My farm is no longer for sale."

The man's face turned red and his mouth rounded in disbelief. For a moment, Faith feared he might explode. And still she held her ground. Then, a movement next to her drew Faith's attention. Anne touched her arm, her smile tentative and shy.

"I…I was wondering, is Adel here today?" Anne asked, her voice low and sweet.

Faith hesitated. "She is, but I'm afraid she's down for her nap right now."

Never in her life had Faith been so grateful to speak the truth. Between the sympathy she felt for Anne and the crestfallen look on the woman's face, Faith almost offered to awaken the child. But she knew she mustn't do that. Before she could say any more, Faith flinched at the sound of Frank's angry voice.

"Would you shut up? Can't you see I'm trying to do a business deal here?" Frank growled at his wife.

Anne backed up in shock, teetering on her cane. Faith cringed, expecting the woman to topple over.

Thankfully, Josiah shot out an arm to steady her and Faith was grateful for his consideration.

"You've got to sell to me," Frank said, not yet finished with his bargaining.

As she looked at the pompous man, Faith couldn't believe what she was hearing. His fists were tightened at his sides and she wondered if he might try to strike her.

"I said no. The place has already been sold. Now, if you'll excuse me, I really must get back to my work."

Turning, she headed toward her watering pot. It took all her nerve not to look back.

As she picked up her bucket and went to refill it, she saw Frank out of her peripheral vision stomping toward his garish truck. Sullen and grumpy, he jerked open the door and pulled himself into the driver's seat. Looking crestfallen, Anne hobbled after him on her cane. Frank didn't even offer to help his wife as she struggled to climb into the high passenger seat. Once again, Josiah offered his aid and the woman blessed him with a smile of gratitude.

Forcing herself to turn away and focus on her work, Faith refused to watch as the couple drove away. She was filled with absolute disgust as she heard the roar of the engine as Frank spun the truck around. The huge tires spat gravel as he gunned it and sped down the lane.

Moments later, Faith lifted her head as the Clarkes reached the county road. When the black truck finally disappeared from view, a heavy rush of air escaped Faith's lips and she breathed with relief.

"When did you sell the farm?" Josiah asked, standing beside her.

She looked at him and realized his expression of disappointment matched Anne's, except for different reasons. Anne had wanted to see Adel but Josiah wanted this farm.

"Actually, I sold it a couple of weeks ago," Faith said.

She held the dented pot with both hands as she tipped it and water cascaded over a green pepper plant.

"But you agreed to give me first option to buy the place," he said, his voice calm but edged with a bit of frustration.

As she set the watering can aside and gazed at his face, she saw the flash of desperation in his eyes and the anguish creasing his forehead. In that moment, she knew he seriously wanted this farm.

"*Ach*, so who did you sell it to?" he asked, a subtle tremor in his voice.

"You! I'm selling it to you," she said, her voice firm with conviction.

And then she was leaving town as fast as she could. Because she couldn't stay here any longer. Anne was getting to be a big problem. If the woman guessed the truth and told her husband, Faith feared what might happen. And she didn't think she'd be able to fight a man like Frank Clarke. He was the type who'd take Adel from her not because he wanted the child, but just to get even with her for refusing to sell her farm to him.

More than that, Faith needed to put some distance between herself and Josiah. Because once he bought her farm, she had no place to go here in Riverton. And she couldn't stand to watch him living here without her. Though it would be more than difficult to leave, it was time for her and Adel to go.

* * *

Josiah stared at Faith, his heart beating madly within his chest. He tried to comprehend what she'd just said but he couldn't grasp it all.

"You…you're selling the farm to me?" he asked, his voice suddenly dry and hoarse.

"*Ja*, I am," she said.

He blinked and swallowed hard, trying to wet his throat. "But…I don't even know if I can afford your price. You still haven't told me what you want for the place."

She turned aside and made a pretense of picking up her empty pot. But not before he saw the shimmer of moisture in her blue eyes.

"It doesn't matter. The place is yours. Whatever you can afford, that's what I'll accept." Her tone was heavy with unshed tears.

"But why? Frank just offered you a ton of money. You could be set for life. Why would you sell it to me?" he asked, taking one step closer.

She took a step back.

"Because I want the farm to go to someone who will honor my *aent* and *onkel*'s memories. I know you'll love and care for this place. I know it'll mean something to you. I won't have it dishonored by someone as hateful as Frank Clarke."

Her voice was filled with conviction and he couldn't blame her. If this were his farm, he'd hate to sell it to a vile man like Frank, too. And yet, her vehemence spoke of something more. Something deep-seated within her heart. She was angry at Frank Clarke and Josiah didn't understand why.

"Did the Realtor in town give you a suggested price?" he asked.

Faith nodded, looking away. "*Ja*, he did. But that doesn't matter anymore. I'll take whatever you can afford. Name the amount and that's what I'll accept."

He told her what he could offer. He'd done a little research of his own and knew what other people were paying locally for their farms. But this place was finer than most, especially after all the work they'd done. He believed his proposal was fair and honest, but it definitely wasn't what Frank Clarke could afford to pay.

"Will that be enough for you and Adel to live on?" he asked. "I don't know where you're planning to go or how you'll make ends stretch, but will you and your *dochder* have enough to meet your needs?"

"*Ja*, I'll make it enough. I'm not afraid of hard work. As soon as you can arrange your money, I'll be ready to sign the title over to you. The sooner the better."

Why was she so eager to leave town? She'd worked so hard to spruce up this place and plant her garden. Yet, she was in a big hurry to go away. It didn't make sense.

Taking a deep breath, he exhaled slowly. There was another topic churning inside his mind and he decided to broach it now. "I've noticed you're uneasy whenever the Clarkes are around."

It was a statement, not a question.

She stepped over the furrow and set the bucket down before picking up a hoe. She didn't look at him. "I don't know what you mean."

Sure she did. Why pretend?

"Is it because Hope used to date their son?" he asked.

"Partly. I also don't like the way Frank treats Anne," she said.

Josiah snorted. "I don't like the way he treats her, either. But it's not our place to interfere. Is…is there any other reason you're so skittish around them?"

She pulled some weeds before smoothing the soil with vigorous jerks of the garden tool. Obviously, she was trying to ignore him as she moved down the long row of radishes that were just beginning to peek up through the dark, rich soil. The ties to her prayer *kapp* fluttered with her energetic movements. Her cheeks were flushed with heat, a pretty shade of pink. And because she refused to meet his gaze, he knew something else was wrong. But what was it?

"I think it's completely understandable why I might act nervous around them. Brian never treated Hope very well. He was abusive. You already know this. He was just like his *vadder*. Mean and cruel. A nasty little man. The last time Brian saw Hope, he nearly…"

Her sentence ended abruptly and she looked up, her eyes wide, her lips tight, as though she'd said too much.

"He nearly what?" Josiah asked, startled by her declaration.

She returned to her chore, jerking hard against the dirt. She waved one hand dismissively at him. "It was a long time ago. Both Brian and Hope are gone and I'd rather forget about it. Now, I've got work to do. Adel will be waking up from her nap soon and I'd like to finish this chore so I can go inside and fix supper."

Taking the hint, Josiah headed toward the barn. A part of him felt jubilant because Faith had promised the farm to him. But another part felt deflated. As soon as he paid the money and they signed the papers to complete the transaction, Faith and her little daughter would leave for good. And right now, Josiah couldn't imagine moving into their farmhouse and working and living here without the two girls around. It just didn't feel right.

As he mucked out the horse stalls, greased the rusty hinges of the barn doors and fed the horses for the evening, he contemplated Faith's words. He'd known Brian had struck Hope a time or two, but nothing critical. Had Brian done something else to cause Faith and her sister to leave four years earlier? And if so, why was it such a secret? Why couldn't Faith tell him about it?

Several hours later, dusk settled over the valley, the sun painting the western mountains with fingers of pink and gray. It was time for Josiah to head out. And yet, more and more, this farm felt like home and he hated to leave. Soon, he'd own the place and he could stay right here.

All alone.

Josiah led his road horse outside the barn to hitch up to his buggy. Faith was striding toward the garden shed. Adel sat facing away from him on the porch swing, rocking her dolly and singing a nonsensical tune. Her child's voice sounded high and sweet, drifting over the evening air like smooth, sugared molasses.

With her hoe, shovel and watering cans in tow, Faith opened the door to the shed. Like always, she cleaned the dirt off her tools, then stored them inside the small structure. On her way to the house, she made a detour over to the water pump, where she rinsed the mud off her hands. She didn't even seem to notice him as he harnessed his horse over by the side of the barn.

As she headed for the house, she called to Adel.

The child hopped off the swing and hurried toward the back door. Josiah waved at them, but neither one saw.

He climbed into the buggy and slapped the leather against the horse's rump. The contraption lurched into motion and he passed by the house. As was his routine, he glanced at the kitchen window, expecting to see Faith standing there as she prepared supper. Tonight, she wasn't there.

The horse trotted onward, pulling the buggy up a slight hill where Josiah turned onto the county road that would take him home. A car came up behind him and he pulled the horse over onto the shoulder of the road as the vehicle whizzed past.

Within ten minutes, he'd be home. His father's farm was only a few miles down the lane. His mom would have food on the table and Josiah could rest for the night. And yet, a heavy weight settled over him like a cloud. A burden he didn't want or comprehend.

He understood Faith's reticence toward the Clarkes. But now, he was convinced her leaving four years earlier had something to do with Brian Clarke. And if it involved Brian, it included Hope, too. So, what had happened between the two? What was so bad that it had compelled the twins to leave town and for Faith to stay away even after Hope's death? Josiah had his suspicions, but nothing was certain. He doubted he could ever convince Faith to tell him the truth.

He felt so torn. Faith had crushed him once and he couldn't let it happen again. Especially since she seemed so determined to leave. He didn't dare trust her with his heart a second time. She would sell her farm to him and leave for good. He would settle in and work the land, eventually taking a wife and raising a *familye* here in

Riverton. It's what he'd always wanted. And Faith would build a life for herself and Adel somewhere far away. They'd be happier apart. He knew it was for the best.

Or was it?

Chapter Ten

"**Y**es, I'm selling my farm to him." Faith jerked her head toward Josiah, who sat beside her in a hard-backed chair.

They were in the real estate office in town and she gazed steadily at Vance Anderson, the agent. It was early afternoon, the day after the Clarkes' visit. Sunlight gleamed through the windowpane. A whoosh of air-conditioning cooled Faith's heated cheeks. The air smelled of burnt coffee. Somewhere down the hall, a persistent beep sounded, followed by hurried footsteps from the receptionist out front. After a moment, the beeping stopped abruptly but laughter and loud chatter filtered in from the outer area. Without a word, Vance stood up from his cluttered desk and quietly closed the door, shutting out the racket.

A middle-aged man with dark hair and graying temples, Vance wore a full beard and mustache. Dressed in creased brown slacks, a leather belt and one of those blue polo shirts the *Englisch* men were fond of wearing, he returned to his seat and glanced at Josiah.

"I'm surprised you sold the farm so soon. I haven't

even had a chance to show the place to anyone yet," Vance said.

"I know, but Josiah will be paying cash," Faith confirmed with a final nod of her head.

Vance's mouth dropped open. "Oh. Well, that should make closing relatively easy."

She caught a hint of disappointment in his hazel eyes.

"Under the circumstances, I don't feel good about charging you my full commission," he continued.

Faith didn't understand and inched forward in her seat. Because she had no idea how long this process of selling her farm would take, she'd dropped Adel off at Sarah Yoder's house on their way into town. Like usual, Josiah had driven the buggy, chatting with the child like they were the best of friends. And Faith supposed they were. Despite her efforts to keep the two apart, they'd become way too attached.

"What do you mean?" Faith asked.

Vance shrugged, his eyes creased with regret. "I haven't even put a for-sale sign in your yard yet. I was coming out this afternoon to do that. Only yesterday, I got the flyers printed off and posted them around town. I've barely done any work to sell your farm and now you've sold it already, almost completely without my help. Under the circumstances, I don't feel good about taking my full commission."

Ah! Now she understood. She'd heard from other members of her congregation that Vance was honest with the Amish. It appeared the rumors were correct.

"I appreciate your integrity, Vance. But you did the research to find out what my place is worth and you've been a good advisor. I need to pay you something for your time," she insisted.

Josiah shifted in his seat but remained silent. The Amish were largely a patriarchal society and she appreciated that he was butting out and letting her handle this. After all, she was still the legal owner.

Out of her peripheral vision, she saw him lift his right hand to grip the armrest. Knowing he was beside her made this whole process much easier. And yet, once they signed the final paperwork, she'd have no excuse to stick around any longer. She'd have to move out of her farmhouse so Josiah could move in. Eventually, he'd marry some sweet Amish girl and raise a family of his own.

Without her and Adel.

"I don't feel good about taking my full commission. How about if I just charge you for my time? Does that sound fair?" Vance asked.

She nodded. "It does. Thank you. So, what's next?"

Twining her fingers together in her lap, she fought off the urge to fidget. She'd never done something like this before and wasn't versed in the process. Though Vance had a reputation with the Amish as someone they could trust, it would be so easy for him to take advantage of her. She was grateful for his honesty.

"I'll contact the title company this afternoon and have them draw up the documents. It'll take them several days to get everything together. Since Josiah is paying cash, there won't be any need for a long, drawn-out credit check. As soon as the money is received by the bank, you can sign the final papers to transfer ownership and you're done," Vance said.

Faith blinked and released a quiet sigh. "It's that simple?"

Vance nodded. "It is when you're paying cash."

His words sounded so decisive. So final. And suddenly, she didn't want to sell her farm to Josiah. Or anyone. She wanted to stay right here in Riverton. It was so hard to let go. She felt disloyal. Like she was losing everyone she'd ever loved all over again. Uncle Noah and Aunt Fern. Hope and her church congregation. Even Josiah. Except for Adel, she had no one left.

Her cousin and church congregation in Ohio had been more than kind and would welcome her back with open arms. There were even several good Amish men who were interested in walking out with her. They liked Adel fine and would make good husbands but it wasn't the same. Selling the farm felt as though she were losing all her childhood memories and her dearest friend in one giant swoop. Yet, she kept telling herself she had no choice. She must take Adel far away where she'd be safe. Especially now that Anne Clarke was aware of the little girl and seemed to like her so much. Leaving was the best thing to do, wasn't it? Of course it was! So, why did Faith feel so rotten about the whole thing?

Determined to do what she believed was right, she turned and faced Josiah. "How long will it take for you to get your finances in order?"

He met her gaze, his eyes filled with concern and something else. Regret, maybe?

This was a time of excitement and joy. He should be delighted to buy such a fine, productive farm. Instead, he looked sad, like her.

"I'll need a couple of weeks. I have most of the money I'll need already in my account. My *vadder* has agreed to give me a loan for the remaining balance. Once I've spoken with him and gathered the funds together, it'll be easy to transfer it to you."

Two weeks. Why did he need so much time? They could transfer the money in one visit to the bank. But Faith didn't argue. Two weeks seemed so long and yet nothing at all. But it would give her more time to enjoy being home. After that, her memories would need to sustain her for the rest of her life. Adel would grow up in Ohio. The child would soon forget about this place. In a year or two, she wouldn't remember Bean or Jack and Tilly. Nor would she recall the fuzzy little chickens they'd bought that day in the feed and grain store. The birds were growing big enough to move out to the coop. Josiah would take care of them. In a few months, he'd pick the apples and harvest the hay and barley. He'd ensure the produce from her vegetable garden was given to the women in their congregation. They'd bottle the food and give enough to Josiah so he would have what he needed for the coming winter. Faith and Adel wouldn't be here for any of those events. Soon, the child wouldn't remember Josiah. Hopefully, Faith would forget about him, too. It was for the best.

Wasn't it?

"Two weeks sounds fine." She glanced at Vance again. "Will that be enough time for the title company to draw up the final papers we need to sign?"

He nodded and smiled wide. "Sure! That's plenty of time. I'll set it into motion. We'll plan to close two weeks from today."

"Thank you," she said.

Coming to her feet, Faith picked up her plain brown purse and stepped over to the door. She needed out of here right now. All she wanted was to collect Adel and go home. For two more weeks, the farm belonged to her. After that, she'd have to rely on the Lord and build a new life somewhere else.

In Ohio.

Josiah joined her as Vance hurried around his desk to shake their hands and accompany them out into the reception area.

"I'll be in touch to let you know where and when our next meeting will take place. I'll need to schedule your closing with the title company first. I can drive out to your farm next week to let you know the details," the man promised.

Faith nodded as Josiah held the exterior door for her. She stepped out on the front step and glanced toward the buggy and horse tied at the end of the street.

As they headed in that direction, she lifted her face into the warm sunshine and inhaled a deep, settling breath. She was highly conscious of Josiah by her side, silent as a tomb. When she stumbled on the boardwalk, he shot out a hand to grip her arm.

"Are you *allrecht*?" he asked, steadying her.

She met his eyes and felt transfixed for several pounding moments. She couldn't move away. Couldn't take a deep breath. For that moment in time, she felt mesmerized and...safe. Then, she pulled away. This wasn't real. She had to take Adel and leave. There was no other way to keep her child safe.

"*Ja*, I'm a bit clumsy but fine," she said.

She gave a shallow laugh, trying to sound casual. She longed to put some distance between them yet wished she could stay right here with him forever. An odd thought, surely. After all, they no longer loved each other anymore. They'd both moved on. Josiah was dating other women and would soon marry. Faith was happy for him. She'd been taking care of herself and Adel in Ohio for several years now. Her ties in Colorado had ended years earlier when she'd turned her back on Josiah and left with her sister. Now she must think about Adel. She would make a new start on her own. She could look after herself. She didn't need anyone. Especially not Josiah, her old school crush. In a few years, she would forget all about him.

Or would she?

Two weeks! That was how much time Josiah had to gather the money he needed to buy Faith's farm. He didn't know why he'd asked for so much time. All he had to do was take his father into town tomorrow morning and they could move the funds within five minutes. Yet, he'd asked for two weeks and he wasn't certain why.

Once the sale was finalized, Faith would move out of the house and leave town. With Adel. A child he'd come to love more than he'd thought possible.

He'd miss the little girl's hugs and smiling face. He'd miss Faith, too. Though he told himself he no longer loved her, she'd always been a good friend. Her work ethic was second to none and he respected her courage in raising her daughter on her own. Maybe she'd made a mistake when she'd had the baby out of wedlock but she was doing right by the child now. There were other things he admired about Faith, too. Things he didn't want to contemplate, especially since she'd be leaving soon.

With the burgeoning crops he'd planted, Josiah should reap a healthy harvest in the fall. Between the apples, barley and hay, he'd have plenty of feed for the livestock he planned to buy, as well as enough cash to live. If all went well, he'd be able to pay his father back within ten years or so. By that time, he'd be completely out of debt and have a wife and children of his own to love. He'd move on in life and be a prosperous farmer. Soon, he'd forget about Faith and Adel.

The thought made his mind go blank. The only woman he could think of was Faith. It seemed odd and crazy, but he felt responsible for her and Adel. Like he was their protector. But he wasn't and they were leaving.

In two weeks.

"Do you…do you need to stop at the grocery store before we head home?" he asked, opening the buggy door and helping Faith climb inside.

"*Ne*, I just want to fetch Adel and go home," she said, not meeting his eyes.

"*Allrecht*, we can do that. Whatever you want," he said.

He went around to the driver's seat and took the leather leads into his grip. After backing the horse up, he directed the animal onto Main Street and they headed outside of town. The rhythmic clop of hooves normally soothed Josiah's frayed nerves. But not today. Instead, the sound was irritating, as though it was pounding out his doom.

He turned onto the county road leading out of town. Another fifteen minutes and they'd be to the bishop's farm, where they'd pick up Adel.

A blue truck came up from behind, hugging close to their back bumper. Josiah hated it when automobiles tailgated him. Urging Bean over as far as he could go, he kept the animal in the traffic lane. He'd heard of speeding vehicles crashing into horses and buggies among his *Gmay*, creating lots of damage and casualties. With a honk of its horn, the truck zipped around them, going way too fast. As a young, less experienced horse, Bean shied and jerked at his harness, then held a steady course along the road. Josiah was pleased by the animal's reaction and grateful when the truck disappeared from view. In time, Bean would get used to honking horns and roaring engines along the roads. He would have been a great road horse for Faith and Adel…if they were staying.

A few minutes later, the buggy crested a hill, then descended into the next valley.

"Guck emol datt!" Faith pointed.

Ahead of them, a blue sedan was parked at an odd angle along the side of the road. It sat next to the turnoff to the Fishers' farmstead, also members of their Amish community. Lying on the ground beside the right front end of the car was the Fishers' overly large mailbox. The box was extra big so it could receive oversized packages from the mailman. No doubt Jakob Fisher had built the box himself, designing and painting it light green, to look like a giant birdhouse. The pine post it had stood on was still in place and it appeared the blue car had struck it, knocking the letter box off its base.

As their buggy approached, Anne Clarke got out of the car with some difficulty, gripping her walking cane as she hobbled over to the broken mailbox. Bending at the waist, she struggled to lift its heavy weight but it didn't budge. Instead, Anne raised one hand to her mouth and looked around, seeming in distress. When she glanced their way, her eyes were wide and tearful.

"It's Anne Clarke. In a blue car," Faith said.

Josiah frowned, wondering why the color of her car was significant. "*Ja*, and I think she's in trouble."

"Do you think she hit the mailbox?" Faith asked.

Josiah nodded. "*Ja*, and I think she needs our help."

Faith heaved a reluctant sigh. "You better stop."

As he pulled Bean and the buggy a safe distance off the side of the road, he thought Faith didn't care much for the Clarkes. They climbed out of the buggy and Josiah's first priority was the safety of Faith and his horse. Reaching up, he took hold of Bean's bridle. The animal danced away, heaving and blowing with agitation.

"There, *bu*. Stand. You're *allrecht*," Josiah soothed.

When he was certain the animal was calm enough not to injure himself, Josiah looked up and found Faith beside him.

"You trained him well. I'll miss him. He's a *gut* horse," she said.

"*Ja*, he sure is."

In unison, they walked over to Anne. The woman gazed at them with wide, tear-filled eyes. She made little gasping sounds, as if trying not to sob.

"Oh, Faith! Can you help me, please?" the woman cried.

"Are you all right?" Josiah asked.

"Yes, I'm fine. But look what I've done."

Anne gestured toward the mailbox and the side-view mirror on her car. It hung limp from the vehicle with nothing but a cable and electrical wire to keep it from falling to the ground.

"What happened?" Faith asked.

"Darrin O'Donnell came up behind me in that ugly blue truck of his and honked his horn. Teenagers shouldn't be allowed to drive, if you ask me. At least, not until they're adults. I was so flustered, I tried to pull over to let him pass. When I did, I hit this mailbox," she said, her eyes brimming with fresh tears.

A rush of sympathy filled Josiah. "That same truck honked and passed us just a few minutes earlier. He startled my horse."

"Yes, Darrin always drives way too fast. Someday, that boy is going to kill someone. Just wait until I share a few words with his mother. That will put a damper on him for sure," Anne said.

With one hand, she dashed tears from her eyes and wiped her nose, looking completely miserable.

Faith leaned over the letter box. "I think it can be fixed, can't it, Josiah?"

Before he could answer, Anne jerked her head toward him, her eyes filled with pleading. "Oh, please don't tell my husband. I'll pay you to repair the mailbox. But if Frank finds out what happened, he…he'll take my driver's license."

The woman's eyes were filled with such despair that Josiah could deny her nothing. Faith stepped close and put her arm around the woman to comfort her.

"There, don't you worry. We won't speak to Frank about what happened," Faith said.

In spite of Faith's seeming animosity toward the Clarkes, Josiah was happy to see she hadn't lost her compassion. But he knew her promise not to tell Frank about the accident wasn't just meant to protect Anne. The Amish preferred to stay out of *Englisch* problems. As a rule, the Amish didn't carry insurance on their homes or buggies and they would never call the police or other *Englisch* authorities unless there was absolutely no other solution. Nor would they speak about this event outside their *Gmay*. It just wasn't their way.

"*Ach*, the mailbox can be restored easily enough. I know the owner and will speak with him today. Don't worry. I can repair the damage," Josiah said.

"Oh, would you? I'll pay you," Anne cried.

"That won't be necessary," Josiah said.

"I'm ever so grateful," Anne said, showing a vague smile of relief.

Faith glanced at the broken side-view mirror on Anne's car. "I'm afraid we can't do anything about that."

Anne studied the mirror for a moment. "I'll take my car to a repair shop in Cañon City and get it fixed tomorrow. Frank is out of town for the next few days and won't even know it was broken."

Wow! Josiah couldn't imagine an Amish wife keeping such a secret from her husband. Lies or half-truths weren't the Amish way. As a people, the Amish abhorred deceit. Josiah had heard that some men abused their wives, children and livestock. He couldn't imagine doing such a thing himself. The idea was completely alien to him.

"All things considered, the damage could have been much worse. There's nothing here that can't be mended," he said, trying to sound upbeat.

"Yes, you're right, of course. But Frank…he always overreacts," Anne said, dabbing at her eyes.

The poor woman. Life must be so difficult for her. But it wasn't Josiah's business and he didn't want to get involved.

"Why don't you go on home now and I'll take care of the mailbox?" Josiah suggested.

Anne nodded, her eyes filled with relief. She turned toward Faith, then tossed a glance at their buggy.

"Is...is Adel with you today?" Anne asked.

Faith's lips suddenly thinned and she folded her arms. Gone was the warm empathy. Now she looked closed and remote.

"No, she's not here." Her words sounded overly clipped.

"Oh, well, I had hoped to see her. She's such a pretty little girl and always makes me smile," Anne confided.

Turning, the woman limped over to the driver's seat of her blue sedan. Josiah accompanied her, ensuring she didn't fall. When she was safely inside and started up the engine, he rejoined Faith.

As Anne pulled back onto the road and drove away, Jakob and Abby Fisher's buggy came from the opposite direction, obviously just returning from town. With a wave, they pulled off on the shoulder of the road and got out. Their children weren't with them.

"What's happened? I saw the car pull away. Are you two *allrecht*?" Jakob asked, looking at his broken postal box.

Josiah explained about the accident as Abby embraced Faith in a consoling hug.

"*Ach*, I'm so glad you weren't involved in a crash. I still remember when Caroline Yoder was in that terrible buggy accident a couple of years ago. It crushed her pelvis and I'm amazed she ever walked again," Abby said.

"*Ja*, she has an indomitable nature. With *Gott*'s help, we can do anything," Jakob said.

Josiah thought about Jakob's words, wishing the Lord would help him find a suitable wife he could love and adore. But the only woman he could think about was Faith. And that ship had sailed long ago.

Jakob crouched down to look at where part of the post was still stuck to the bottom of the mailbox. "It doesn't look too serious. You don't need to fix it for me, Josiah. I'll take care of the repairs."

"Are you sure?" Josiah asked, feeling doubtful.

Jakob flashed a wide smile and waved a hand in the air. "*Ja*, I'll just pull out a couple of nails to remove the broken wood and reaffix the mailbox to its post. It'll be good as new. No big deal."

Josiah nodded, grateful for good friends. His Amish *Gmay* shared more than just a common belief in God. It also consisted of people he could depend upon in times of need. He would never consider calling a tow truck or *Englisch* repairman. Not when he had members of his *Gmay* to call upon.

Faith seemed eager to get back in the buggy and continue their journey home. Josiah ensured there was no debris lying in the road, then waved farewell to the Fishers. On the ride to the bishop's farm to pick up Adel, he sat quietly on the bench seat with Faith.

"You seemed on much friendlier terms with Anne today," Josiah said, trying to make conversation.

She looked away but not before he saw a brief flash of bitterness in her eyes and voice. "We're not friends. We never will be."

"I guess not," he said. But he didn't understand.

Why was she so uneasy around the woman? The accident today was a foolish mistake. Josiah could understand Faith's animosity toward Frank Clarke. But why was she so against Anne? Other than poor driving, the woman was harmless enough. There was no reason for Faith to dislike her so much.

Or was there?

A sudden idea flashed through Josiah's mind but he shook it off. The thought seemed too far-fetched and improbable. It would be better to focus on picking up Adel and getting her and Faith home, then move the money he needed to buy her land. In two weeks' time, they would close on the farm and Faith would leave town with her little girl. Josiah's life would settle into a quiet, boring routine. No more getting up super early so he could help his father with chores before driving over to Faith's farm to work for her. No more hearing her sweet laughter as she played in the yard with Adel, or the child's shrieks of joy as she chased the fuzzy little chickens around the barn. No more helping Faith water her tomato plants or weed her cabbage patch.

Correction.

His tomato plants and cabbages. His horse and buggy. Or at least they would be in two weeks. Buying the farm so Faith and her little girl could leave town was for the best. It was what Josiah wanted, his dream come true.

Or was it?

Chapter Eleven

The following Tuesday, Faith ran out of milk. As a growing child, it seemed Adel was a vacuum for the stuff. Since she didn't have a cow of her own, Faith would have to drive into town.

Again.

Fearing she might bump into Anne Clarke, Faith asked Josiah to watch Adel for her. She didn't dare take the child with her again. Since Adel was down for her afternoon nap, it wasn't a big deal. Josiah shouldn't even have to speak with her.

Everything went according to plan. Inside the grocery store, Faith moved quickly and with purpose, trying not to draw attention. As she paid the bill, she thought she'd gone without notice. Within minutes, she'd be back in her buggy and on her way home. And never again would she return to town, except to sign papers at the title office and hop a bus back to Ohio. But just as she stepped outside onto the boardwalk, Anne intercepted her. How did the woman always seem to know when she was here? It was almost as if Anne had a spy inside the store who tattled on Faith.

Minutes after the chance meeting, Faith raced to her buggy, backed the horse away from the hitching rail and slapped the leads against Bean's rump to urge him into a breakneck trot out of town. Anne's words to her had left Faith shocked and badly shaken. The woman knew Faith's secret! Two weeks was too long to remain here in Riverton. She needed to pack up Adel and leave right now.

Today.

As she pulled into her farmyard, Faith drew the flustered horse to a halt in front of the spacious barn. Flinging open the door to the buggy, Faith jumped out and leaned against the conveyance. Her arms and legs wobbled. She took several deep, cleansing breaths, trying to calm her racing heart. Now that she was home, she could relax a bit.

For the time being.

Still trembling, Faith reached up and clasped Bean's halter before leading the horse into the barn.

"There, Bean. I'm sorry to make you hurry so fast." She soothed the anxious gelding by rubbing his face and neck. The animal swished his tail and snorted, as if he understood her motives for making him rush home.

Faith's hands shook as she struggled to unhitch the buggy. She'd get the horse taken care of first, then go inside the house and pack her and Adel's bags as quickly as possible…

"Here! Let me do that."

She whirled around and bumped into Josiah. Taking the stubborn buckle from her hands, he released the catch with ease, then reached to remove the breast collar from around Bean's neck.

"Adel hasn't made a peep the entire time you've

been gone. She's still asleep," he said, seemingly unaware of Faith's distress.

"That's *gut*," she said.

With quick jerks, Faith opened the buggy door, reached inside for the gallon of milk, then slammed the door closed.

Bean jerked at the loud noise and danced away.

"There, *bu*. Stand!" Josiah held Bean still as he reached to pat the animal's neck.

In the next moment, Josiah glanced in surprise at his damp palm before looking at Faith with a bit of accusation in his eyes.

A frown creased Josiah's high forehead and his eyes narrowed in bewilderment. "The horse is wet with sweat and seems overly jittery. Did he suffer a fright on the way home?"

Faith cringed, unable to respond. She hadn't meant to drive Bean so hard. She'd just been desperate to get home as fast as possible.

When she didn't speak, Josiah repeated his question, his voice infinitely soft and nonaccusatory.

"Did everything go all right in town?"

"*Ja*, everything's fine. I…I was planning to rub the horse down. I wouldn't put him away all lathered like this," she said.

She reached for the currycombs sitting on a shelf. Before she could administer to Bean, Josiah took the brushes from her hands.

"I'll care for the horse. Why don't you go inside and check on Adel?" he said.

His kindness was just what she needed. Until she knew her child was safe, she felt as though she might explode.

"Danke!"

Turning, she scurried toward the back porch, conscious of Josiah staring after her in curiosity. She could almost feel his gaze drilling a hole in her back. Instead of being so nice, she wished he would yell at her for abusing Bean. But shouting had never been Josiah's way.

Inside the house, she hurried to Adel's room and peeked in at the child. Adel lay upon her little bed, covered by her special blanket. Hope had pieced the pink-and-gray fabric together and quilted it herself before Adel's birth. Though the cloth was getting worn from overuse, it was still Adel's favorite.

The child lay on her side, her eyes closed, her rosebud lips slightly parted in repose, innocent and sweet. She had absolutely no idea her birth had created so much turmoil.

Backing away, Faith silently returned to the kitchen. Within minutes, Josiah stepped inside, careful not to let the screen door clap closed and awaken the child.

It was on the tip of Faith's tongue to tell him to go away and leave her alone, but she couldn't do that. Not after the many kindnesses he'd shown her. In spite of her abandoning him four years earlier, he'd done so much to help her. Even now, during her greatest crisis, he was there for her.

She busied herself by lifting the gallon of milk off the table and reaching for the fridge door. Josiah quickly tugged it open before stepping aside so she could slide the milk inside.

"Danke," she whispered, her throat suddenly overly tight.

"Are you *allrecht*?" he asked, his face filled with genuine concern.

"Of course." She stepped back, tugging at the ties on her black traveling bonnet. Anything to occupy her so she wouldn't have to meet his eyes.

"Have you…have you and your *vadder* had a chance to move the money yet?" she asked, desperate to sign the farm over to him and leave town.

He stepped near. "*Ne*, we were planning to do that tomorrow, or the next day. Why the sudden rush? What has upset you?"

Her back was to the sink and his tall frame blocked her escape. She felt boxed in. Trapped!

"I…I just think it's best if we go to the title company first thing tomorrow morning. Then, Adel and I can catch an afternoon bus out of town," she said, determined not to lie.

He stared at her in confusion. "But I thought it was agreed we would sign everything in two weeks. Why are you suddenly in such a hurry to get it done now?"

She didn't know how to respond. Not without telling him what had happened in town with Anne Clarke.

Looking up, she saw a myriad of emotions flashing within his eyes. Bewilderment, pain and something else she couldn't quite put her finger on. Suspicion, perhaps?

She turned aside, praying he didn't guess the truth. Pulling at her bonnet ties, she realized the strings were now securely bound in a solid loop. She jerked the head covering off and fidgeted with the knot.

"*Ach*, I can't believe this," she muttered under her breath.

"Faith." Josiah placed his hand on her arm, stilling her movements.

Gently, he took the bonnet and set it aside before returning his attention to her. She gazed into his eyes, filled with a strong yearning for…what?

"Was Anne Clarke in town again?" he asked, his question calm and passive.

"*Ja*, she was there," Faith said, her voice a tight squeak.

"And did the two of you speak?" he asked.

Staring at the clean floor, she felt her eyes flood with hot tears as she nodded.

"And that upset you?" he asked.

Another nod.

"Has she guessed that Hope and Brian are Adel's parents?" he asked.

She jerked her head up, her mouth dropping open in surprise. "How…how did you know?"

Oh, no! She shouldn't have said that. Her foolish words had just confirmed what he'd guessed at. But she'd never been good at keeping secrets. Not from this man.

Memories flashed through her mind as she recalled every time her twin sister had made her promise not to tell anyone about her worldly escapades with Brian Clarke. The moment Faith got with Josiah, he noticed she was troubled by something and she ended up blabbing everything to him. This time, she'd kept the secret of Adel's birth for four long years. Now the truth was out. There was no turning back.

"I…I have to get out of here," she whispered, her voice sounding hoarse with unshed tears.

She flinched when he reached up and gently cupped

her cheek with his hand. Before she could stop herself, she turned her face into the warmth of his palm. She was so weary of the subterfuge. So tired of feeling frightened all the time. And now that he knew the truth, she was both terrified and relieved at the same time.

"Oh, Josiah. How did you guess?" she asked.

"I know you pretty well. I can always tell when you're nervous about something. I can read your body language and understand your facial expressions," he said.

She shook her head, not wanting to believe him. "That's not possible. You couldn't know about Hope and Adel just from looking at me."

He reached out and enfolded her hand in his, holding her prisoner there.

"I saw other signs as well," he said. "Before you left town, I hadn't proposed to you yet, but we'd discussed marriage. You even said you loved me, and I loved you. But if you were Adel's *mudder*, you would have had to be unfaithful to me before you left town with your sister. And I just don't believe you're the kind of woman to ever do that."

His voice cracked and so did her heart.

"*Ne*, I would never cheat on you," she whispered. "But I still don't think that's enough for you to guess that Hope is Adel's *mudder*."

He cleared his throat. "I also watched you whenever we encountered the Clarkes. You're downright skittish around them. At first, I thought it was because they're *Englisch* and Brian used to hit Hope. But then I realized it was something more. From that, I've pieced a few things together."

Her lips parted as her breathing quickened. She

didn't know what to say. She couldn't think clearly. And suddenly, she just burst into tears and the whole sordid story poured out. She told him everything, including the fact that her name was on Adel's birth certificate. He heard it all.

"Then today, Anne confronted me in town," she said. "I didn't confirm any of it, but she knows Brian is Adel's *vadder.*"

Josiah tilted his head to one side in that endearing manner of his that said he was curious about something. "How could she have guessed?"

Faith pressed her fingertips to her mouth, trying to gather her composure. Fresh tears squeezed from her eyes and trickled down her cheeks. When she thought about what Anne had told her, it seemed quite poignant to her.

"Anne said she could see her son in Adel's little face," she said.

Josiah showed a sad smile. "*Ja,* there is a slight resemblance. Adel has Hope's eyes and forehead, but she has Brian's mouth and jaw."

"She does?" Faith stared at him, thinking he must be daft. Whenever she looked at the child, all she could see was a miniature of her twin sister.

He nodded. "*Ja,* she does."

Slowly, he reached out and gently pulled Faith into his arms. She didn't stop him. Heaven help her, she couldn't pull away to save her life.

She gazed up into his eyes, lost in their dark depths. For so long, she'd carried this awful secret in her heart, guarding it at all costs. To protect Hope's child, Faith had denied her deepest desires and abandoned her own love. She'd do almost anything to keep Adel safe.

"Faith." He lowered his face to hers and kissed her. A soft, gentle caress that spoke volumes.

She breathed him in, wishing she could stay there forever. Then, she remembered who he was and who she was and that Adel was still in jeopardy.

Drawing away, she pressed the palms of her hands against Josiah's solid chest and stepped around him. For good measure, she placed a wooden chair between them and brushed the tears from her eyes. She must be strong and do what was right for Adel. She must!

"Please let me go," she said.

She'd done it now. If only she'd kept her silence a bit longer. Then she'd be out of here and Adel would be safe. She should have denied the whole thing, but lies went against the tenets of her faith. Her willpower had been worn down and she'd spoken out loud what she'd vowed to never tell anyone, especially the man she'd once loved and abandoned. And now that he knew the truth, she was terrified. She had so much to lose. She had to leave as quickly as possible. Because if she didn't, she'd lose Adel for good. And not even Josiah could stop it from happening.

Josiah stared at Faith, watching a variety of emotions cross her face. Relief, fear and, finally, absolute panic. For so long, he'd been hurt and angry, wondering why Faith would leave him like that without an explanation. Then he'd feared someone might have taken advantage of her. Now that he knew the truth, he was relieved no one had hurt her, yet he felt heartbroken that she hadn't confided in him.

She didn't trust him.

"Once you left town with Hope, why didn't you

write and tell me where you were? I could have helped," he said.

"How? There was nothing you could do. We didn't want Brian to find out where we'd gone. We needed to get Hope far away from him. Then, when Hope discovered she was going to have a *boppli*, we had an even greater reason to keep our location secret," she said.

"You didn't trust me? You didn't think you could tell me?" he asked, feeling crushed.

She shrugged her slender shoulders. "It wasn't your burden, Josiah. My duty was to look after Hope and Adel. I didn't want you to have to lie to your parents if they asked."

He took a deep inhale, then let it go. He understood her reasons but it still hurt. Because of Hope's foolish mistakes, they'd lost four years of their life together.

"Please don't tell anyone what you know, Josiah. I'm begging you. Please keep this to yourself. If Frank Clarke finds out the truth, he'll sue me for custody. He doesn't care about Adel. He'd do it just to be mean. And in a custody case, *Aent* Fern's attorney told me, grandparents often take precedence over an *aent*. I'd lose Adel and she'd be taken by the Clarkes and raised *Englisch*."

Josiah winced. "Why do you think Frank could win a custody suit? You've already told me your name is on Adel's birth certificate."

"*Ja*, but what if Frank were to demand a paternity test? *Aent* Fern's attorney told me that, because I'm Hope's identical twin, a test would prove inconclusive for Adel's *mudder*. But it would prove that Brian is Adel's *vadder*. And you know Frank hates being told no. He'd take Adel from me just because he can," Faith cried.

Tears ran down her face. Ah, how he hated to see her cry. He reached to pull her into his arms again, to comfort her, but she moved away.

She was right, of course. Frank Clarke had the wealth and power to take Adel. The thought of little Adel growing up in an abusive household with *Englischers* was horrifying. Especially since Adel had known nothing but an Amish way of life. Josiah loved Adel. Even though Frank was the child's biological grandfather, Josiah didn't want to see her taken away from Faith. Lots of people had children but that didn't mean they made good parents. And Faith was Adel's aunt. She was also an exceptional mother.

"Did Anne threaten to take Adel from you?" Josiah asked.

Faith shook her head. "*Ne*, just the opposite. She insists she doesn't want Frank to know the truth. She's the one who said if Frank knew, he'd try to take Adel from me. Anne acknowledged that she had to raise Brian in an abusive home. She thinks that's why he became so mean like Frank. He learned it from his *vadder*. With her bad leg, Anne says she's too old and lame to raise another child now. She insists she doesn't want to take Adel from me."

Hmm. This didn't make sense. If Anne didn't want Adel, then what was the problem?

"*Ach*, then why worry? If Anne isn't a threat, there's no reason to go," he said.

Faith released a small, guttural laugh. "There is still a risk. Don't you see, Josiah? What happens if Anne slips up and tells Frank what she knows? Or what if, maybe a year or two from now, Anne changes her mind and decides she wants to take Adel from me?"

Ah! Now he understood.

"So, you think Anne might change her mind one day?" he asked.

Faith nodded. "*Ja*, that's what I fear more than anything."

"You know fear is the thief of faith. Fear and faith can't coexist. Why not trust the Lord instead?" he asked.

She huffed and reached for her laundry basket sitting nearby. With stiff jerks, she shook out articles of clothing and folded each one, laying them in tidy piles on the large, clean kitchen table.

She didn't look at him. "You make it all sound so simple. And it's not. I can't afford to take chances. Not with Adel."

"What will you do, then?" he asked.

"*Ach*, I'll take Adel far away where the Clarkes can never find us," she said.

So, that was it. She'd made up her mind. She was leaving. For good this time.

"Back to Akron?" Josiah asked.

Faith froze, then laid one of little Adel's dresses and an apron on the table. She turned to look at him. "How... how did you know that's where we were staying? Surely my facial expressions didn't give that away, too."

He shrugged. "It's simple."

She inclined her head. "It is?"

"Of course. You might recall that I know some of your *familye* came from Indiana and some from Millersburg, Ohio. I even wrote the bishops there to ask if they knew you."

"You did?"

"*Ja*, and they wrote back to say they did not. But when you mentioned your cousin bottled dilly beans, I remembered you have a widowed second cousin living in Akron. You mentioned her a time or two when we were kids. She was ten years older than you but you really liked her. I then realized that was where you must have gone. I just wish I had thought of it sooner. Then, I would have come to find you."

Her forehead crinkled. "You would?"

"*Ja*, in a minute. But it didn't occur to me until you mentioned the dilly beans. And when I understood that Adel was born eight months after you left Riverton, I finally realized you couldn't be her *mudder*."

"Oh," she said.

A deafening silence filled the room. It lasted an infinitely long time. Faith seemed lost in her thoughts and Josiah didn't interrupt her. He wanted all of this to sink in. She needed to figure out that she needed help. That she could trust him.

"*Ach*, I guess I won't be returning to Ohio, then," Faith finally said.

Josiah released a heavy sigh, realizing he'd been holding his breath. A sick feeling settled in his gut but he forced himself to keep his patience.

"Then, where will you go?" he asked, knowing he couldn't force her to stay. It would have to be her choice.

She jerked her head up, her eyes filled with sadness. "Somewhere else. It doesn't matter, as long as I can keep Adel with me."

He took a step closer, speaking gently. "It matters to me."

She took a step back. "*Ne*, Josiah. Don't say that. I've got to leave and Adel is going with me. Please don't try to stop me. I promised Hope I'd keep her safe. I can't let my sister down."

The last thing he wanted was to chase her off. He held perfectly still, using soothing persuasion instead. "Why not take Anne at her word? She said she doesn't want to take Adel from you. She's a woman in her late sixties and has an injured leg. She can't raise a young child by herself. You don't need to go away."

"But Anne and Frank have lots of money," she said. "They could hire a nanny for Adel. Anne wouldn't have to raise her on her own. And the thought of Adel growing up in a household with people who don't love and care about her makes me crazy. I can't even think about such a horrible thing."

"Anne has lost a lot, too. Would it be so bad to let her get to know her granddaughter?"

Fresh tears welled in her eyes. She looked so miserable that he longed to take her into his arms. He resisted the urge.

"It's not that simple," she said. "If I let Anne start spending time with Adel, Frank will hear about it and become curious. He would soon guess the truth and then I'd lose her for *gut.*"

"You've always been a woman of faith. Instead of fretting and stewing over things that haven't happened yet, why not trust in *Gott* and exercise your faith now?" he asked.

She snorted. "I wish it were that easy."

"It is. Everything will work out fine. All you have to do is believe. The Lord will make a way for you and Adel to be together forever and remain here in your home, too. I know He will!"

A flash of hope filled her eyes. "Do you really think so?"

He nodded, determined to put his trust in *Gott*. Because without faith, he had nothing at all. At least, nothing that mattered to him.

"I do. I believe it with all my heart," he said with conviction.

She gazed out the kitchen window, looking with such longing at the fields where hay and barley were burgeoning in the fertile soil. By end of summer, he planned to buy some more horses to train and cattle, pigs and goats, too. They'd worked so hard to bring this place back to life. They were only a few months away from reaping what they'd sown. The harvest was within their reach. If only Faith and Adel would remain here, maybe they could mend their broken relationship. Maybe they had a chance...

"I don't see how it can end well for Adel, but I'll try not to leave town just yet," Faith said. "At least, not until we've signed the final papers with the title company."

A laugh of relief burst from his lips. "That's *gut*! I'll speak with my *vadder* and we'll go to the bank first thing tomorrow morning and transfer the money. In the meantime, I hope you won't worry. You're not alone, Faith. I'm here for you. So is *Gott*. I hope you believe that."

She gave a shuddering sigh, seeming calmer now that they had a plan. They could make this work. He was certain of it.

Finally, she nodded. "*Allrecht*, I'll try to wait one more day."

Try. He didn't like that word but figured it was the best he was going to get right now.

He stepped over to the threshold and gripped the doorknob. "I'll see you tomorrow morning, then. Once

I'm finished at the bank, I'll stop by and pick you up and we can ride together to the title office."

As she looked at him, she lifted her chin slightly higher, seeming to gather her courage around her. "*Ja*, tomorrow."

He left, walking out to the barn, where he forced himself to finish his chores for the day. It was all he could do to keep from racing back to the farmhouse, taking Faith into his arms and confessing that he'd reached a new realization today. He didn't want her to go. In spite of all the pain and anguish he'd suffered over the past four years, he didn't want to lose her again. And though she'd agreed to wait one more day, he knew she was only postponing the inevitable. She was going to leave. And he couldn't stop her.

Ah, he felt so confused. He thought he didn't love her anymore. Now he needed time to sort out his feelings. Anger, heartache and compassion warred inside his brain. Though he understood Faith's reasons for disappearing all those years earlier, it still hurt. He knew she couldn't take chances with Hope's baby. She'd made so many sacrifices to keep her sister's child safe. But hadn't he deserved at least one letter from her? Hadn't their love mattered enough to at least say goodbye?

Securing the barn door, he stepped outside and climbed inside his buggy. The evening sky was darkening. It was time to go home.

As he pulled out of the farmyard, he knew he had to forgive Faith. She'd been frightened and worried and he wished he could have been there for her. Now he had to figure out a way to convince her to stay here in Riverton permanently. He had one day to do it in.

Because once she left, Josiah doubted he'd be able to find her again. If he couldn't convince her that Adel would be safe here, he knew they would leave. And when they did, they would take his shattered heart with them. For good this time.

Chapter Twelve

The following morning, Faith knelt on the floor beside her bed and pulled out her battered brown suitcase. Thinking she should start packing, she hesitated, running her fingertips over the worn zipper. Like most Amish, she and Adel had few worldly possessions. Just this farm and a few pots and pans. All their clothes would easily fit inside this one bag. When they'd come here a couple of months ago, Faith hadn't expected much. Then, she'd discovered her aunt had left everything to her. By Amish standards, Faith was now a wealthy woman. But money didn't matter to her. She wanted a place to call her own. A *familye* and someone to love. And for just a few moments, she let herself hope that maybe…

No! She couldn't remain here. It did no good to even contemplate staying. Her situation was impossible. But she'd told Josiah she'd try not to leave just yet. Against her better judgment, she'd promised to wait awhile longer. She just hoped she didn't regret that decision.

Pushing the case back underneath her bed, she stood and dusted off her long skirts. It was early yet and she'd just fed Adel her breakfast. The girl was now playing quietly in her room. Soon, Josiah would pull his buggy into her farmyard and they'd drive into town. He was going to move his money first, then pick up her and Adel. They'd go to the title office and sign the final documents, transferring ownership of the farm to him. After that, Faith could make concrete arrangements to go…somewhere. Everything was working out as she'd planned. And yet, she felt horrible inside. Like her world was caving in on her and she couldn't escape.

As she stepped into the living room, the subtle sound of a car engine caught her attention. Peering out the wide window, she saw Anne Clarke's blue sedan pulling into her yard.

Oh, no! What was the woman doing here? Why wouldn't she leave them alone?

Hurrying to the front door, Faith stepped outside quietly before the woman could knock. She didn't want Adel to hear Anne and come running. If the child discovered that Faith wasn't her real mother…

Faith shook her head. She couldn't think about that, either. She had to get Anne to leave them alone. But how? Faith couldn't lie. So, what could she say? What could she do?

Murmuring a little prayer for help, she stood on the front step and waited for the woman to get out of her car. When she saw how Anne struggled to stand and walk with the aid of her cane, a wave of compassion enveloped Faith. She headed down the narrow path and met the woman at the edge of the gravel. Anne found her balance, so Faith didn't go any farther. Instead, she rested her hands on the gate, keeping it closed, using it as a silent barrier between her and the other woman.

"Hello, Faith!" Anne smiled but then winced in pain as her ankle rolled beneath her.

Faith gasped, thinking to run and help her. Anne held up her hand as she regained her footing. "I'm fine. No need to fuss over me."

"Are you all right?" Faith asked.

Anne nodded, taking a deep inhale, as if her exertions were almost more than she could bear. "I just need a moment to catch my breath and let the pain ease. My doctor tells me I'll need a wheelchair one day but I keep fighting it off."

Before she could stop herself, Faith flung open the gate and stepped over to take the woman's arm, offering her support. "Let me get you a chair."

"No, I'm not staying that long." Anne stood straight and licked her upper lip before releasing a huff of resignation.

"Why have you come?" Faith asked, folding her arms.

Faith's upbringing told her that she should take the woman inside her house. She should offer her a warm biscuit smoothed with creamy butter and a glass of freshly squeezed orange juice. But Adel was inside. And welcoming Brian Clarke's mother into her home seemed much too personal. Too intimate and… dangerous. But more and more, Faith was struggling to retain her animosity toward this woman. She just couldn't do it anymore.

"I…I came to apologize to you," Anne said.

Faith inclined her head, feeling confused. "You did? What for?"

"I fear I may have upset you yesterday. I didn't mean to frighten you, Faith," she said.

"I'm fine. Think nothing of it," Faith said, trying to calm her pounding pulse.

"Well, it's not fine. I know how much you love Adel. But imagine how I feel, too. That first time I saw your little girl and realized she must be Brian's daughter, I was in shock. Brian was my only baby. My son. For two years, I've mourned his death. I know he was just like Frank, but he was my baby and I loved him. And then, to discover he has a living, breathing child of his own staying right here in our community, it was almost more than I could comprehend. I had to see more of Adel. I had to get to know her," she said.

Faith's breath caught in her throat. How could she respond honestly without confirming the truth? Her voice wobbled. "Adel is my little girl. Mine alone."

"I know. You're her mommy and I don't want to take her from you. I'm sorry for just blurting out that I'd guessed the truth. I didn't mean to frighten you, Faith. It's just that I wanted to see her so badly. You see, I miss Brian more than I can say. Adel looks a lot like him and she even tilts her head the same way my son used to do. Even though Hope didn't marry Brian, at least she gave us this precious gift. I'll always love Hope and be grateful to her for that."

Oh, dear. This was Faith's worst nightmare come to life. Her thoughts scattered. She didn't know how to react. For a moment, she wished Josiah was here. He'd know what to say, what to do. With his calming words, he always eased the tension in every difficult situation. But he wasn't here. Faith was alone.

"Hope died several years ago. Adel is my child," Faith insisted again.

It wasn't a lie, after all. Faith was Adel's mommy now. Nothing else mattered.

"I know. We've both endured a lot of pain. I've lost my son and you've lost your sister. Now I have nothing," Anne said, biting back a raw sob.

Faith's heart squeezed hard but she didn't say a word. She didn't dare. Looking at the woman with what she hoped was a kind but resolute face, she bit her tongue and forced herself not to confirm Anne's assumptions. Faith had to be careful what she said. No matter what, she must put Adel's safety first.

"You still have your husband. You have Frank," Faith said, her voice gentle.

Gripping her cane, Anne snorted and impatiently dashed the tears away from her cheeks with her free hand. "I lost Frank years ago. All he cares about is money and bossing everyone around. I have no one."

Her words sounded so sad and hollow. So lonely. If not for Adel, Faith could end up the same way. All alone. But maybe she could make a difference for this poor, distraught woman right now.

"That's not true. You have the Lord. Jesus Christ is the redeemer of all mankind. Because of Him, the grave holds no power over any of us. Through His Atonement, we will all see our loved ones again someday. Life ends in this frail world, but there is so much more to look forward to, for each of us. One day, you'll see Brian again, and I know I'll see Hope again. This is what I believe," Faith said.

Anne sniffed and wiped her nose, her eyes filled with hope. "Do you really think so?"

"I do." Faith gave a firm nod of her head.

"I...I want to believe that, too. You see? We're not so different after all," Anne said.

Faith showed a tight smile, feeling empathy for Anne. Through no fault of her own, she'd lost her beloved son and still had to cope with an abusive husband. But they weren't alike. Anne was *Englisch* and Faith was Amish. They lived completely different lives and believed different things. They were worlds apart.

Or were they? Maybe in their fundamental belief in Jesus Christ and the healing power of His love, they weren't so different after all. Not if they were really trying to follow the Savior.

"I'm so glad. Now I really must get back to my work." Faith turned toward the house.

"You...you're not angry with me?" Anne asked.

Faith glanced at the woman. Anne's eyes glistened with fresh tears, her expression so contrite that Faith didn't have the heart to reject her.

"No, Anne. I'm not angry with you. None of this is our fault. We're both innocent, and yet we now must decide how we will proceed. For me, I will do my best to follow Christ."

Faith meant every word. She was, however, afraid of Anne and what she could do if she decided to fight for Adel.

Anne gave a shuddering sigh. "Oh, I'm so glad. I've watched you and Josiah together with Adel. You make such a sweet family. You're both so loving and caring and that's all I want for that little girl. A compassionate home where she can grow up and be happy."

A memory of seeing Anne's blue car parked up on the county road flashed through Faith's mind. If Faith and Adel remained here in Riverton, would the woman continue to spy on them?

"Yes, I love my child deeply. But it's rather creepy for you to watch us with your binoculars. I'd prefer you not watch us like that anymore. I'm sure you can understand why it's upsetting to me. You might frighten Adel," Faith said, hoping the woman would comprehend and go away and leave them alone.

"Of course! I don't want to scare Adel," Anne exclaimed. "I promise it won't happen again. It was just that once, when I wasn't certain if Adel was Brian's daughter. When we see each other in town, would you mind if I talk to her for a few minutes?"

Faith hesitated and Anne hurried on...

"Just as friends. I don't want anything more from you. I...I'm not in any condition to raise another child anyway. I'm old and lame now. Knowing how much you love her, I'd rather Adel were raised by you."

"Yes, you said that yesterday," Faith said, feeling threatened.

"Well, I meant it." Anne spoke gently but with passion. "I'd die before telling Frank about her. I think you already know my husband isn't a nice man. I just would like to speak with Adel now and then. It doesn't go against your Amish faith or anything, does it?"

Faith didn't know what to say. Like yesterday at the grocery store, the woman's request startled her. A sick feeling settled in Faith's stomach and left her trembling. She had spent the past three years protecting Adel. She couldn't let down her guard for even a moment. But Faith's Amish upbringing insisted she be kind to others. That she trust in *Gott*. She wanted to show compassion toward Anne, but she didn't dare get too close.

"You can always speak to us. But please don't come out here to my home without an invitation. It's not right. Some of my Amish people might see you here and get the wrong idea," Faith said.

It was true, after all. The last thing she wanted was for people in her congregation to think she was becoming *Englisch*.

Anne nodded. "Okay, I won't. I promise."

"Good!" Faith stepped away, hinting the woman should leave.

"Thank you, Faith. Thank you for taking such good care of Adel," Anne said.

"Of course. She's my child. I take the best care of her that I can," Faith said.

Anne nodded and turned toward her car. Faith breathed a silent sigh of relief. Finally! Finally, the woman was leaving. But as Anne hobbled over to her vehicle and climbed inside, Faith felt suddenly empty. She stood there and didn't move as Anne started up the engine, turned the big car around and pulled slowly out of the driveway.

Glancing at the farmhouse, Faith hurried up the walkway. After stepping inside, she locked the dead bolt and went straight to her room. Kneeling on the floor again, she jerked the battered suitcase out and tossed it on the bed. The old mattress bounced with the impact.

She and Adel had to leave town. Right now. This very moment.

She was frantically pulling clothes out of the dresser drawers when Adel came in and gazed at her with wide, curious eyes.

"Where you go, *Mammi*?" the child asked, clutching Martha to her chest.

"We're going on another little trip, sweetums. In just a few minutes, I'll pack your things, too," Faith said, trying to keep her voice light and cheerful.

"*Ne*, I not go. I stay with Bean and Ziah."

Faith glanced absentmindedly at the girl. Her focus was on packing, not her disobedient child. "Adel, it's time to go. We can't stay."

"*Ja*, we stay."

"I said *ne*. Now, go and get your clothes out of your room, please," Faith said.

"*Ne!* I not go. I hate you!"

Before Faith could stop her, Adel raced into her bedroom and slammed the door hard.

Staring after the girl, Faith dropped down onto the bed, holding a pair of black stockings in her hands. It felt as if a sharp knife had just stabbed her chest. When she'd come here with Adel a couple of months ago, Faith never would have believed the girl would become so attached to the farm, or to Josiah.

Looking around the room, Faith noticed the freshly painted walls, the simple, sparse furnishings, and the small window on the far wall. As a child, she'd shared this room with Hope, lying beneath the warm covers late at night as they'd giggled and schemed about how wonderful their lives were going to be when they grew up. They would both marry tall, handsome Amish men, work hard and have prosperous neighboring farms close together. Each of them would raise a passel of children and they'd visit one another regularly. They'd grow old sharing one another's joys and sorrows. They'd always be with each other no matter what. Twin sisters, tied together.

Forever.

Now Hope was gone. Cut down in her youth. All Faith had left of her was Adel. And Faith wasn't about to lose her child, no matter what Anne promised her.

Hopping off the bed, Faith finished her packing. Then, she crossed the hall and quietly entered Adel's room. The little girl sat curled in one corner of the room, cradling Martha in her arms, her face turned against the wall.

Faith sat on the bed, keeping her voice soft and gentle. "Dilly bean, I'm sorry we quarreled. Can we talk about this, please?"

Before she could say anything more, Adel launched herself into Faith's arms and cried.

"I'n sorry, *Mammi*. I not hate you. I lub you," the girl said.

Holding her tight, Faith closed her eyes and let her emotions wash over her. Old hurts evaporated when she thought about how much she adored this little girl. And she imagined this was how her Heavenly Father felt when His children disobeyed His commandments. But He'd lovingly provided a Savior, so they could repent and return to Him.

"*Ach*, and I love you too, *Liebchen*. I always will. No matter what," Faith said.

She hated to drag the child away from her new home but thought it was best. Soon, Adel would forget about this place, Bean and Josiah. But leaving would be the hardest thing Faith had ever done. Because she wouldn't be coming back. Nor would she miss just the farm. She was also going to miss Josiah more than she could say. Against her better judgment, she'd fallen in love with him again. Perhaps she'd never stopped loving him. It didn't matter anymore. Because either way, she was going to lose him all over again. For good this time.

It was done. The money had been transferred. Josiah stepped out of the bank and glanced up at the early-morning sky. Not a single cloud and no wind, either. Perfect for spraying his barley crop for aphids. But that would have to wait until later this afternoon.

He should be happy. Within the next couple of hours, he'd be the new owner of Faith's farm. It was a fine place. And yet, a feeling of gloom settled inside his chest and he couldn't shake it off.

"I thought you said you were headed over to Faith's place to pick up her and Adel."

Josiah turned and found his father standing beside him. John Brenneman had accompanied Josiah into town so they could move the money to buy Faith's farm. Though Josiah had accumulated most of the funds he needed, he was now in debt to his father. He'd pay off the loan over the next ten years, something he knew he could manage, as long as he worked hard and his crops produced well. Never would he default on his own father, even if it meant he must take on extra construction jobs here in town to pay the bills. He would pay back every penny, no matter how long it took.

"I am. I'm going there now," Josiah said.

The two men had driven their own horses and buggies into town. That way, John could head home to his work while Josiah drove over to get the two girls. Then they'd go to the title office. Later tonight, Josiah's mother was planning an extra-special supper to celebrate. Josiah planned to invite Faith and Adel to attend. And yet, knowing Faith and Adel would be leaving soon, Josiah wasn't in a festive mood.

It was still early, barely eight thirty. He'd stood with his father on the bank's doorstep promptly when it opened that morning. The transaction had taken no more than twenty minutes. Now all that was left was to sign the final documents. Then, Josiah would be the new owner of a fine, productive farm.

He'd also be completely and utterly alone.

"Maybe Faith misunderstood your plans," John said.

Tilting his head to one side, Josiah gazed at his father in confusion. "What do you mean?"

John pointed down the road. Heading toward them on the boardwalk was Bishop Yoder. The man was walking fast, his gaze pinned on them. And beyond him at the end of the street, Faith was just pulling into the bus depot. She was driving her horse and buggy at breakneck speed. Josiah caught barely a glimpse of her and Adel as they entered the parking lot and disappeared from view.

Blinking in confusion, Josiah glanced at his father as the bishop joined them. Then Josiah closed his eyes for several moments as realization washed over him.

"She's doing a runner," Josiah whispered beneath his breath.

"*Ach*, I'm glad I found you," Bishop Yoder said, gasping for breath.

"*Guder mariye*, Bishop. What's put you in such a big rush?" John asked.

"I was hurrying to my buggy when I saw you standing here." The bishop jerked his head in a sharp nod toward the bus depot.

All three of them turned and stared that way, as if they expected the building to suddenly explode. Josiah didn't know what to think. When he'd spoken to Faith yesterday afternoon, they'd agreed he would pick her and Adel up this morning. They had a plan and she'd seemed perfectly calm. Had he misunderstood their arrangement? Obviously something had happened to make her change her mind. That's all that made sense.

"I was just coming out of the feed and grain store when Faith blasted past me in her buggy," the bishop said. "I waved but she didn't notice me. She looked rather frightened and preoccupied. Earlier, I was in the grocery store and Anne Clarke came in while I was there. I overheard her telling Marlin Thompson that she'd just been out to Faith's farm. Now I see that Faith has gone to the bus depot with little Adel, and I fear the worst."

A feeling of dread washed over Josiah. "*Ach*, you're right to be concerned. This doesn't look *gut*."

He knew Faith was more than frightened of the Clarkes. Yesterday, Josiah had talked her down. He'd smoothed things over and reassured her that everything would be okay. She'd promised to try and wait another day. But something had obviously changed. Anne had been out to visit Faith this morning. At her farm. And Josiah had no doubt that meant just one thing...

"She's running away," the bishop said.

Josiah's heart sank. A feeling of absolute panic overwhelmed him. It was as if he had only minutes left to live.

"Why would she do that?" John asked, his forehead crinkled in confusion.

Josiah and Bishop Yoder shared a look but didn't explain. They both knew what had spurred Faith to leave.

John rested a hand on Josiah's shoulder. "I don't know what's going on, but you go after her, *sohn*. Faith belongs here in Riverton with you. Bring her and Adel back."

What? John couldn't know the truth about Adel's birth. Josiah certainly hadn't told him anything.

John showed a smile of reassurance. "I don't know what all has transpired between you and Faith but I see what a hard worker she is. I also see the way you look at each other when you don't know someone's watching."

The bishop chuckled. "*Ja*, I see it, too. You two were meant for each other. Go to her. Make sure she's not leaving town. Bring her back and we'll plan an early wedding," the bishop said.

Josiah blinked. "I…I don't know what you mean. Faith and I aren't engaged. We're not…"

His voice trailed off and the bishop released an impatient huff, then closed his eyes for a moment, as if gathering his patience so he could explain a simple idea to a wayward child.

"*Ja*, you know exactly what we mean," Bishop Yoder said. "You and Faith love each other. You just need to tell one another that. Forgive and forget the past. Take her hand and walk into the future. It's bright and *gut*. This is where Faith and Adel belong. Here with you."

"*Ach*, the bishop's right," John said. "Marry that girl, *sohn*. You already have a fine farm to live on. Now you just need a wife and *bopplin* of your own. Go and get them. Bring them home."

Home. What a sweet word. But it would never be

complete without Faith and Adel living there, too. Josiah knew that now.

Looking at the two men, he saw the strong urgency in their eyes. Knowing his own father supported him and agreed with the bishop that he should marry Faith did something to Josiah inside. It galvanized his feelings for her like never before.

He loved her. He couldn't deny it any longer. Maybe he'd never stopped. He'd been hurt when she left. But knowing her reasons for leaving, he couldn't begrudge what she'd done. And if she really was about to buy a ticket out of town, he'd better act quick. Because he couldn't lose her again.

"I...I've got to go." Turning, Josiah sprinted down the street.

As he ran, he wasn't winded at all. In fact, he felt as if he could fly. Never had he felt so free and happy. So filled with hope.

He heard the two men laughing behind him.

"*Ach*, young love," one of them said.

Josiah wasn't certain, but he thought that was his father's voice. Knowing the two men wanted him to marry Faith meant a lot. It meant everything. But what if Faith refused to come home with him? The problem with Anne Clarke hadn't been resolved. Faith was frightened and desperate to keep Adel safe.

As he passed the series of shops and the post office on Main Street, Josiah's mind raced. Once he got to the bus depot, what could he say to induce Faith to believe everything would work out for the best? That Anne would keep her word and not try to take Adel away. That they should be together and Adel would always remain at home with them.

Josiah carried a prayer in his heart, determined to accept nothing less than Faith and Adel being with him. He just hoped he could persuade Faith to believe it was the right choice, too. No matter what, he had to find a way.

Chapter Thirteen

Faith lifted Adel out of the buggy and adjusted the child's black traveling bonnet. Though it was still early in the day, a car whizzed by on Main Street, and Cliff Packer, the postmaster, was sweeping the front steps to his business. The air held a hint of sage and damp earth. No doubt it was raining up in the Wet Mountains, which meant they'd have a storm here in town by early afternoon. That would be great for Faith's garden and fields. But she wouldn't be here to see the plants flourish. She couldn't stay.

"*Ach, Mammi*, we not leave Bean," Adel said, her eyes crinkled with worry as she gazed at her beloved horse.

Faith reached inside the buggy for their bags before closing the door. "Don't you worry, sweetums. He'll be fine. I've parked him in the shade and I'll make sure someone fetches Josiah to retrieve him later today."

Adel cast a dubious frown at the drab brick depot.

"I not go," the girl murmured.

Faith took the girl's hand, trying to keep her voice happy and positive. "I thought you liked traveling on the bus. We'll have another fun adventure."

"*Ne*, I stay here. I want Bean and Ziah," Adel said, shaking her head.

Faith almost burst into tears. This situation was bad enough without facing Adel's upset, too. She felt guilty for causing her child pain by taking her away from a home they both cherished.

Setting the suitcase and her purse on the gray pavement, Faith crouched down and took the girl into her arms. "I know, *Liebchen*. I wish we could stay. But please know that I'm doing what I believe is best for both of us. I really need you to trust me right now. Can you do that, sweetheart? Please?"

Meeting the child's eyes, Faith noticed Adel's quizzical frown. Then the girl tilted her head to one side.

"Are we leaving 'cause of Anne?" Adel asked.

Faith stiffened. Adel was so observant. But how could she know? Faith had caught the child eavesdropping a time or two. Surely she hadn't overheard any of her conversations with Anne or Josiah. Or had she?

"Wh-what do you mean?" Faith asked.

Adel shrugged. "Anne's nice. I like her, *Mammi*. But she make you unhappy."

Unhappy? How perceptive.

"That's just because she's *Englisch*. She's not Amish, like us. They're not our people," Faith said.

"*Ja*, but Anne's nice, *Mammi*. She not hurt us. You not worry. I protect you." Adel wrapped her little arms around Faith's shoulders and pulled her close for a tight squeeze.

Faith tried to swallow but her throat felt like sandpaper and her heart turned a series of somersaults in her chest. She couldn't believe Adel was trying to protect her.

Faith kissed her daughter's cheek. "*Danke*, sweet-ums. I'm so glad I have you to watch out for me. But we have the Lord to do that, too. He's always with us, no matter how difficult life might become. We have to believe that."

Adel quirked her eyebrows in a startled question. "Then, why we leave?"

Oh! Faith almost groaned out loud. This child was way too smart for her own good. But what did she expect? Hope had always been very bright too, and this was Hope's child.

Faith was such a hypocrite. The fact that Adel was right left her feeling ashamed and deficient. Here she was, telling her child to have faith, yet she wasn't setting a very good example for the little girl. She needed to exercise faith and show Adel that she trusted the Lord in all things. But if she stayed, she might lose the girl.

"We…we need to go check on Cousin Sadie. Remember she's all alone, like us. We've been gone a long time and I want to visit her in Ohio," Faith said.

There. That was good. It was partly true. Though Sadie belonged to an Amish community who looked after her and ensured her harvests were brought in, she was a widow and lived by herself. Faith loved Sadie and wanted to see that she was doing okay. But maybe returning to Ohio wasn't such a good idea anymore. Josiah knew where they'd been staying for the past four years and the Clarkes might find out and come looking for them there.

No, Josiah wouldn't tell anyone where they were. He would never do anything to hurt her or Adel. Faith could trust him. She knew that now. She loved him. So much that, if she thought about it for long, she might load Adel back into the buggy and return home...where she'd face the fallout with grim determination.

"I want Ziah," Adel said, her chin quivering and her eyes glistening with moisture.

Oh, no! Not tears. Faith could stand Adel's worst tantrums but she hated it when the child cried.

"I know! We'll send him a letter. *Komm* on, let's go inside. You can help me write to him," Faith said.

Giving Adel no time to argue, Faith took the child's hand, picked up her bags and led the girl inside the bus depot. The reception counter sat at the front of the waiting area with a bench seat and a number of chairs for people to sit on farther back inside. The drab gray walls looked as though they hadn't been painted in years and the air smelled of burnt popcorn.

Doyle, a bald-headed *Englisch* man Faith knew from previous experience, sat behind the counter. He leaned back in a rolling chair, his feet crossed at the ankles as he rested them up on the top of the desk. Munching on a glazed doughnut, he held a coffee mug in his free hand. Upon seeing her, he quickly lowered his feet, set the doughnut and mug aside, and cleared his throat.

"Ahum, howdy there. Can I help you?" he asked, standing behind the glass pane.

Before Faith could respond, Adel cried out in delight and hurried over to several brightly colored candy machines sitting beside the main door.

"*Mammi*, I want sweets," she said, speaking in *Deitsch*.

It was barely eight thirty in the morning and the girl hadn't eaten much breakfast.

Feeling distracted, Faith shook her head. "Not right now, *Liebchen*. Maybe after lunch."

"Ahh!" Adel grouched, gazing at the machines with longing.

Faith stepped up to the reception desk and snapped open her plain brown purse. "I'd like to buy two tickets, please."

Doyle rested his hands on a computer keyboard. "Where to?"

Faith hesitated. Should she return to Ohio? Or go somewhere else? Maybe she should go to Denver, just to get out of town fast. Then she could decide where to go from there. She wasn't about to abandon her Amish faith. Knowing how the grapevine worked, she realized if she went to her father's people in Indiana, her new bishop would write to Bishop Yoder here in Riverton. She trusted Bishop Yoder but there was no way she could hide completely and she hated this feeling of deception. But right now, she wanted to go anywhere, just to put some distance between Adel and the Clarkes.

"To Denver, please," she said.

Doyle lifted his eyebrows in query. "One-way?"

"Yes, please," she said, her heart up in her throat.

Her stomach felt as though she'd swallowed a hive of bees. Everything within her rebelled at what she was doing. She didn't want to go but what choice did she have? She couldn't stay and take the chance that Anne would come knocking on her door again. Or what if the Clarkes sent the police after her? This could turn ugly really fast.

Doyle nodded and rang up the bill. With reticence, Faith paid the sum, and he handed over the tickets. She then asked if he could send word to Josiah Brenneman that he needed to come retrieve Bean and her buggy from the parking lot.

Doyle frowned at that. "Yeah, I get off work in a few hours and can stop by your farm to let him know. Your bus leaves at ten thirty, so you've got a little wait."

Two hours! It felt as if Faith's lungs sank down to her toes. What if one of her Amish people saw Bean standing in the parking lot and came over to check it out? Or worse—what if Anne Clarke drove by and recognized her buggy? Or someone in the grocery store called the woman to tell her Faith and Adel were here?

Well, it was the chance Faith would have to take.

Maybe she'd buy the candy for Adel after all. She hated to bribe the child but two hours was a long time for an antsy toddler to wait around without some kind of distraction.

Taking the tickets in her trembling hand, Faith collected Adel and went to the back to sit on the hard chairs and wait. She remembered four years earlier when Aunt Fern had brought her and Hope to this same station and bought them one-way tickets to Ohio. They'd been fleeing town then, too. And all of a sudden, Faith hated the thought of running away. Especially since she hadn't yet signed over the farm to Josiah. But it couldn't be helped. She told herself she'd contact him once she got Adel somewhere safe. Wherever she ended up, she could sign the papers from there and transfer ownership over to him. Or maybe she could leave Adel with her cousin and return to Riverton, just long enough to finalize the paperwork. Somehow, she'd make it work.

Remembering how she'd left last time without any word of farewell to Josiah, she pulled out a pen and notebook and started writing a letter to him. Adel helped for a few minutes, drawing him a picture of Bean and their buggy tied up at the bus station. But soon, the girl lost interest and played quietly with Martha.

As Faith wrote the words and explained why she must leave so abruptly, she wasn't sure what to say without revealing her true feelings for him. Though she had two hours to wait, she didn't dare go looking for him, mostly because she knew he'd try to talk her out of leaving. But she had to let him know of her plans. He deserved that much. Four years earlier, she'd left without a single word of explanation.

No doubt he was at her place right now, knocking on her door, expecting her to go to the title office with him to sign over her farm. This time, she couldn't abandon him without some kind of apology. After all his kindness to her and Adel, he deserved so much more. She had to at least write him a letter to say a final goodbye.

Faith tried to write the words, but her hand shook and nothing came out. So many feelings washed over her and she didn't know what to say. She looked up and froze.

Josiah! He was here. Standing in the doorway, his gaze resting heavily on her. His dark eyes were filled with a mixture of sadness, disbelief and…what else? Relief, maybe?

"Ziah!"

Adel dropped Martha on the floor and raced over to the man. He scooped her into his arms and lifted her high in the air. The child squealed with delight.

"I knew you'd *komm*, Ziah. I knew it," Adel said.

"Dilly bean!" He called her nickname with lively energy, then pulled her close for a warm hug.

Faith stood abruptly and dropped her pen with a clatter. The pages of her unfinished letter fluttered to the floor. Seeing him here did something to her inside. It was like the sun had been blocked for years and had just come out from behind the mountains and every warming ray now rested squarely on top of her head. Her joy at seeing him was unimaginable. She couldn't begin to express how she felt.

"Josiah! Wh-what are you doing here?" she asked, her voice an emotional squeak.

Carrying Adel in his arms, he walked over to her, his eyes never wavering from hers.

Faith glanced nervously at the reception counter but noticed Doyle had stepped into the back room, giving them some privacy.

"My *vadder* and I were just coming out of the bank after moving the money and I was ready to head over to your farm. That's when I saw Bishop Yoder hurrying toward me. Imagine my surprise when I noticed you pulling into the bus depot," he said.

"Oh," she said, closing her eyes tight for several moments as she ducked her face down toward the floor.

In a burst of flame, she realized what her pulling into town like that must have looked like. A flush of heat filled her cheeks with embarrassment. She'd been driving way too fast. John Brenneman, Bishop Yoder and Josiah had all seen her pulling into the bus depot. What they must think of her, she could only imagine.

"Where are you going?" Josiah asked, his voice soft and gentle.

Lifting her head, she met his gaze. In his eyes, she saw mild curiosity and serene acceptance. How she wished he would yell and scream at her instead. At least then she'd know how to react. But right now, she felt confused, mortified and…

Lost.

"I'm sorry, Josiah. I…I was writing you a letter to explain." She gestured to the paper scattered on the floor.

"Explain what?" he asked, seeming perfectly calm.

"I… We have to leave. Right now…"

He lifted a hand, shushing her words. With gentle movements, he set Adel on her feet and took her over to the candy machines. He retrieved several quarters from his pocket. Faith heard the soft murmur of his voice as he spoke to Adel, but with their backs to her, Faith couldn't hear their words.

She watched in silence as Josiah placed some coins into the machines, then twisted the knob and cupped his hand beneath the spout to collect the pieces of candy. Pouring the sweets into a clean kerchief, he took Adel over to a chair in the farthest corner where Faith could still see her. Adel sat down to enjoy her treats. Josiah returned to Faith and indicated that she should join him on the bench. When they were settled, he turned to face her and lifted one muscular arm to rest against the back of her chair. His full attention was leveled on her.

"Now, tell me what's going on," he said.

In a rush, the story poured out of her. How Anne Clarke had driven out to her farm early that morning and how frightened she was of the woman.

"I thought Anne told you she didn't want to take Adel from you," Josiah said.

"She did, but what if she changes her mind? She came to my farm, Josiah. What if she does it again and someone sees her there? They might guess the truth, too. Don't you see? I've got to take Adel away from here."

"Okay, where are we going?" He came to his feet.

She stared up at him. "What do you mean? You're not going with us."

"*Ja*, I am."

"But...why would you do that?" she asked.

"Because I lost you once and I won't lose you again. I'm in love with you, Faith. I was so hurt when you left me the last time but now I understand why you went away. And if you're leaving again, then I'm going with you. I won't be left behind this time."

She stood and gazed at his face, seeing the determination written there. "But you belong here. You have your *familye* and a farm of your own to run. As soon as I get settled, I'll sign it over to you, Josiah. It's yours. Your life is here."

"*Ja*, my parents are here and so is your farm. But you won't be. So, I would have nothing. You are my life. If I stayed, I'd be living on that big farm all alone. And I won't do that. Not ever again. If you're leaving, Faith, then so am I."

She dropped her mouth open, trying to sort out what he was saying. Trying to understand.

"You...you love me?" she asked.

He laughed. "*Ja*, I do. And my home is with you and Adel. So, tell me where we're going and I'll buy my ticket and we'll leave right now. Today. No looking back. My *vadder* will see to the harvest of your fields and you can sell the place to Frank Clarke and we'll buy our own place somewhere else, far away from here."

"You...you'd really do that?" she asked.

He nodded, his eyes filled with resolute purpose. "*Ja*, I'd really do that."

"Oh, Josiah! We can't leave. But I can't stay. I don't know what to do." She pressed her fingertips to her lips and looked away, unable to meet his eyes. A huge tear ran down her cheek and she wiped it away impatiently.

He stepped close and took her into her arms and, heaven help her, she let him. She couldn't fight him anymore. Not when he was everything she'd ever wanted.

He spoke against her ear. "You're not going to lose Adel. Not ever! Have a little faith and trust in the Lord."

He was right, of course. She couldn't run and hide forever. She must trust in *Gott*. All she'd ever wanted was to come home and be with Josiah.

A little hand reached up and took hold of hers, and Faith was jerked back to reality. She looked down as Adel hugged against her leg.

"I'n not lost, *Mammi*. I'n right here. I'n your dilly bean and no one else's," the girl said.

Faith gave a shuddering laugh and reached down to pull the child up into her arms. "Oh, Adel. I love you so much."

Josiah enfolded them both in his strong arms. As he looked at Adel, he pretended to be hurt by her words. "You won't be my dilly bean, too?"

Adel's forehead creased in thought, then she relented and smiled wide as she wrapped one arm around his neck. "*Allrecht*, Ziah. I be your dilly too, but no one else's."

They laughed and Faith had to wipe the tears from her eyes. And suddenly, she found herself being squashed in a three-way hug.

As Josiah looked deep into her eyes, he whispered the words Faith so longed to hear.

"I love you, Faith. And I love Adel. Nothing matters more to me than the two of you," he said.

Their noses touched as Faith met his eyes. "And I love you, Josiah. I always have. I always will."

He smiled wide. "Then, marry me, sweetheart. Marry me and make me the happiest man in the world. I promise to spend the rest of my life protecting and loving you and Adel."

Faith hesitated for just a moment too long.

"Say *ja, Mammi*. I wanna go home now," Adel cried.

A joyous laugh burst from Faith's lips and she nodded. "*Ja, ja*, I'll marry you. I can't fight the both of you. And honestly, I don't want to anymore."

He kissed her then. A passionate kiss that was filled with warmth and love. For the first time in her life, Faith didn't care who saw them.

When they drew apart, Josiah took the tickets she'd set on the bench next to her purse. Lifting her suitcase, he walked over to the reception desk and asked for a refund.

Doyle just smiled and nodded and handed back the money. Then, hand in hand, they stepped out of the station and headed over to where Bean was dozing in the warmth of the day.

"*Ach*, we'll be married as soon as possible," Josiah said, his voice filled with exuberance.

Faith looked up and saw John Brenneman and Bishop Yoder walking toward them and nodded, feeling light of heart and happier than she could ever remember.

"*Ja*, just as soon as we can," she said.

Filled with faith, they greeted Josiah's father and the bishop. Faith stood back and smiled as Josiah explained what they planned to do. She didn't need to say a word. Not when Josiah said it all. They had found their forever home and were ready to face whatever the future might bring. Together.

Epilogue

6 Years Later

"*Grossmammi! Grossmammi!*"

Faith turned at Adel's happy cry and saw the girl sprinting toward the county road. The early-October air was crisp and fragrant with the aroma of freshly cut hay. Josiah had mowed it just yesterday, the last to be brought in. Over the next handful of weeks, they would complete their apple harvest. Faith had been bottling all the produce she could get out of her vegetable garden. Between that and the potatoes they'd dug up, they would have plenty to eat during the coming winter. Now she would put up apples for homemade pies and applesauce. All was safely gathered in. This was a time of plenty, a time of joy. A time to celebrate family and the coming holidays.

And a new baby before Christmas.

Waddling over to the graveled driveway, Faith lifted one hand to shield her eyes from the piercing sun. It was just beginning to peek over the eastern mountains, chasing the morning dew off the verdant green grass in the front yard. She rested her other hand on her large abdomen, feeling Josiah's baby kicking vigorously within her. Already, she could see a line of Amish horses and buggies trotting along the county road as they made their way to her farm, where they would hold church services, greet friends and *familye*, and worship *Gott*.

Faith gazed at the turnoff as a blue sedan turned onto the dirt road, then inched its way slowly toward her house. Adel sprinted toward the car. At the age of nine years, her legs were long and strong and she was undoubtedly thrilled to see her grandmother again. It was nice that Anne came to Faith's home each Sabbath day, to share the word of *Gott* and Sunday dinner with them.

Correction! This was now Josiah's farm, too. Faith still couldn't believe they'd been married almost six years. The time had flown by and so much had happened since their wedding day. Speaking of which…

Where was her husband? He'd been here minutes earlier, setting up long tables and chairs for the lunch they would share with their congregation once church services ended.

Resting a hand on her distended middle, Faith gasped when her unborn baby thrust a foot hard against her ribs. It was such a strong child that Faith thought he must be another boy.

"*Mammi!* Wook at me!"

Faith swiveled around and smiled. Her little three-year-old Benuel was on the swing in the backyard, being pushed by his five-year-old sister, Sarah, who had been named after the bishop's wife. Two of her three beautiful children…soon to be four.

"Higher, Sarah. Push higher," Benuel cried as he gripped the handles and pumped his legs hard.

Faith laughed, filled with such gratitude for the wonderful *familye* the Lord had seen fit to send to her and Josiah. Except for good health for each of them, she could ask for nothing more.

"That's *wundervoll, sohn.* But don't go too high this time," Faith warned.

"Don't worry, *Mammi.* I won't let him," Sarah called.

Dear Sarah. Her young voice sounded so mature. So much like the calm assurance Josiah was known for. No matter what craziness was going on in their lives, he always knew just what to say in that soothing tone of his. And Faith was grateful at least one of her kids had taken after him.

Benuel was so fearless. The boy still had a scab on his chin from the last time he'd gone too high on the swing. But after having a good cry and letting her put salve on the scrape, he'd jumped up and run off to do it again. He was so much like Hope that Faith wondered if the child had been born to the wrong mother.

And just like that, tears burned the backs of Faith's eyes. Now that she was expecting her fourth baby, it seemed more and more that she was always thinking about her sister. How she wished Hope was here to watch Adel grow up. She longed to share sweet sentiments as well as the concerns and joys of life with her dear sister. But Hope was long gone. Now Faith could only trust in *Gott* and believe that she would one day see Hope again in the next life.

Glancing at the road again, Faith folded her arms and gazed at Adel. The girl looked so much like her mother. So prim and proper in her light blue dress, pristine black apron and white prayer *kapp*. They each wore their best clothes today for church. Using Aunt Fern's old sad iron by heating it on the woodstove, Adel had pressed all their clothing yesterday. The girl was so diligent and wise.

"I think you would be pleased with her, Hope. At least, I know I am. I pray I've done you proud in how I've raised her." Faith whispered the words, as if Hope were standing right beside her, listening to everything she said.

She stepped over to the walk path and waited. A mild breeze blew in from the south, pushing fall leaves of gold, orange and brown across the front lawn. Adel fidgeted nervously beside the flower bed as Anne pulled up in front of the house and killed the engine to her car. Faith would have gone to assist the woman but there was no need. Adel was more than capable of helping her grandmother.

The girl opened the car door and took the wooden cane Anne handed to her. Then, Adel offered her arm as Anne stepped out awkwardly and leaned heavily against the child, giving her a warm hug.

"Oh, it's so good to see you, sweetheart. How have you been?" Anne asked.

"*Gut!* How are you, *Grossmammi*?" Adel returned.

"I'm good," Anne said, before lifting an arm to wave at Faith.

"*Hallo!* And *willkomm*," Faith called.

She watched silently as her daughter and the *Englisch* woman walked arm in arm toward the barn, where they would soon hold church services.

"What are you thinking so hard about?" A strong arm

suddenly curved around Faith's waist and she whirled around to find Josiah standing beside her.

"*Ach*, there you are," she said, patting his solid chest with the palm of her hand.

He leaned down and nuzzled her neck, pressing a warm kiss there. "*Ja*, here I am. Were you looking for me?"

She swatted at his shoulder, pretending to be outraged by his forward actions.

"Stop that. The whole congregation is almost here and someone might see."

She jutted her chin toward the dirt road where the line of buggies were starting their descent down to their farm. Soon, their property would be overrun with Amish families lining up to go inside their barn and listen to their minister preach the word of *Gott*.

He chuckled but behaved himself for the moment. His face was slightly red from his earlier exertions.

"Did you finish putting up the tables and chairs?" she asked.

"*Ja.*" He nodded.

"You could have waited. The men are just now arriving and would have helped you. Remember! Many hands make light work."

"It was no trouble." He glanced down at her obvious pregnancy. "Did you need me for something? Are you feeling *allrecht*?"

"*Ja*, I'm fine. I was just wondering where you were," she said.

"I'm right here, sweetheart. I'll always be right here," he said, giving her a tight squeeze.

As he wrapped his arms around her, she leaned against his side, letting him hold her steady. She drank in this quiet moment with deep, satisfied breaths. In her heart, she felt more content than ever before in her life. She'd lost so many beloved family members, and yet the Lord had given her so much in return.

"I was just thinking how blessed I am," she said.

He slid his large hand over her rounded belly, his voice a reverent whisper. "I was thinking the same thing. *Ich liebe dich*."

"And I love you," she said, smiling with contentment.

He kissed her, then jutted his chin toward Adel and Anne. "They're happy together."

She nodded but frowned. "Do you think we did the right thing by telling Adel the truth?"

Though Faith didn't look at him, she felt Josiah's nod. "I do. Frank's been dead almost three years now. The heart attack was rather sudden but he's no longer a threat to any of us. And I think knowing the truth is *gut* for both Anne and Adel."

A deep sigh escaped Faith's lips. "*Ja*, but Anne now has a lot of money at her disposal. You don't think she'd ever change her mind and try to take Adel from us, do you?"

He snorted. "*Ne*, I don't. Even when Frank was alive, Anne kept her word. She never told a single soul what she knew. And now that he's been gone so long, she's done nothing but be supportive to us. I think you blessed her life by telling Adel that she's her *grossmudder*. And since Frank's death, Anne hasn't missed a single church service. She finally has the freedom to live and do as she wants. It's a nice way to honor Hope's memory."

Faith nodded. "*Ja*, I like that."

He was right, of course. In her heart, Faith knew if Anne wanted to take Adel from her, she would have done something about it before now, before the child was old enough to resent her for any perceived wrong-doings. Now it was too late. Adel was fast becoming a young woman and had memories of a loving house-hold here on the farm. And although Anne had told Faith she wasn't interested in becoming Amish, she always honored Adel's plain heritage. Because Hope was Adel's mother and had been Amish, too.

In addition to attending church with them, Anne frequently joined their quilting bees, fundraisers and socials. Anne spent every single holiday with Faith's *familye* and she'd even assisted with the births of Faith's other two children. At least, as much as she could. She was not only a grandmother to Adel, but to Sarah and Benuel as well. But there was an extra-special bond between Anne and Adel. Anne had lost her son and Adel had lost Hope. But they always had each other. Truly, the truth had set them all free.

Faith felt at peace. Her decision to exercise faith and remain here in Riverton with Josiah hadn't been easy but it had been so worth it.

"Faith! Josiah! *Hallo!*"

Looking toward the south pasture, Faith saw the line of buggies pulling up and parking expertly next to each other. Surrounded by her tall children, Sarah Yoder waved at them before retrieving a large wicker basket that was no doubt filled with food for their afternoon feast.

Teenaged boys hopped out of the buggies and began unhitching each horse without being asked. They knew their job so well as they turned the animals loose into the pasture with Bean and Billy. The old gelding lifted his head and pranced toward the other horses, as if greeting good friends. He'd outlived his life span and Faith would hate it when he died.

Sarah and Benuel came running from the backyard, hurrying over to greet their friends.

To welcome the congregation, Faith waggled her fingers at Sarah and heaved a deep sigh. "I guess I better get back into the kitchen. I've got several more pies to cut. The bishop will be wanting to start services soon."

She turned to go but Josiah held her tight. "Wait for the other women to join us and they can do it. I want you to take it easy…at least until your due date."

She patted his hand, grateful to have someone in the world who loved and cared about her. "Don't worry. I feel fine."

He frowned. "I just don't want you to go into early labor, like you did with Benuel."

She nodded, remembering the birth of their son. When she'd gone into early labor, Lovina Lapp, their midwife, had barely made it in time. In spite of losing her twin sister to childbirth, Faith hadn't been frightened at all. Because now she had Josiah and the Lord. Her faith sustained her these days, in all things.

She gazed lovingly at her three children: Adel, Sarah and Benuel. Soon, there would be a fourth. Boy or girl, it didn't matter to Faith. *Gott* had been so good to her. So kind and generous. Her precious *familye* was more than she'd ever imagined. More than she'd dared hope for. And Josiah, the love of her life.

No, except for another healthy child, she couldn't ask for anything more.

* * * * *

If you enjoyed this Secret Amish Babies story, be sure to pick up the previous books in Leigh Bale's miniseries:

The Midwife's Christmas Wish
Her Forbidden Amish Child
An Amish Christmas Wish

Available now from Love Inspired!

Dear Reader,

Years ago, I learned a terrible secret about a child-hood friend whom I cared deeply about. I knew the pain, humiliation and embarrassment my friend would feel if her secret was revealed to others. A short time later, my friend and I had a falling-out. It took almost a year for us to reconcile. When we did, she confided that she had been terrified I might reveal her secret to everyone, just to be spiteful. But honestly, that thought never entered my mind.

Looking back on that time, I've often wondered why I didn't tell the secret to everyone. I could have deeply hurt my friend and possibly made it impossible for her to attend school again. But I never wanted to hurt someone else like that on purpose. I always had a deep, abiding faith in the healing power of the Atonement of Jesus Christ, so I chose instead to forget about my friend's secret and let her resolve it in her own way.

Now that I'm a grown woman, I realize my friend's secret was not so serious after all. But it was to her. And she had to figure out how to resolve it and how to move past it on her own. Each of us faces the same di-lemma in our own lives. Big or small, our troubles can all be resolved by turning to the Savior, Jesus Christ. He paid the ultimate price for each of us and can make all our problems right in the end. Because of Christ's eternal sacrifice, there is no burden, no sadness, no crisis, that is too great for Him to cure. When we trust our Heavenly Father and turn to Him in humility, He can work wonders in each of our lives. This is what I know and believe.

I hope you enjoyed reading this story and I invite you to visit my website at www.LeighBale.com to learn more about my books.

May you find peace in the Lord's words!
Leigh Bale

THE TEACHER'S CHRISTMAS SECRET
Seven Amish Sisters • by Emma Miller

Cora Koffman dreams of being a teacher. But the job is given to newcomer Tobit Lapp instead. When an injury forces the handsome widower to seek out Cora's help, can they get along for the sake of the students? Or will his secret ruin the holidays?

TRUSTING HER AMISH RIVAL
Bird-in-Hand Brides • by Jackie Stef

Shy Leah Fisher runs her own bakery shop in town. When an opportunity to expand her business comes from childhood bully Silas Riehl, she reluctantly agrees to the partnership. They try to keep things professional, but will their past get in the way?

A COMPANION FOR CHRISTMAS
K-9 Companions • by Lee Tobin McClain

When her Christmas wedding gets canceled, first-grade teacher Kelly Walsh takes a house-sitting gig with her therapy dog on the outskirts of town for a much-needed break. Then her late sister's ex-boyfriend, Alec Wilkins, unexpectedly arrives with his toddler daughter, and this holiday refuge could become something more...

REDEEMING THE COWBOY
Stone River Ranch • by Lisa Jordan

After his rodeo career is ruined, cowboy Barrett Stone did not expect to be working with Piper Healy, his late best friend's wife, on his family's ranch. She blames him for her husband's death. Can he prove he's more than the reckless cowboy she used to know?

FINDING THEIR CHRISTMAS HOME
by Donna Gartshore

Returning home after years abroad, Jenny Powell is eager to spend the holidays with her grandmother at their family home. Then she discovers that old flame David Hart is staying there with his twin girls as well. Could it be the second chance that neither of them knew they needed?

THEIR SURPRISE SECOND CHANCE
by Lindi Peterson

Widower Adam Hawk is figuring out how to parent his young daughter when an old love, Nicole St. John, returns unexpectedly—with a fully grown child he never knew he had. Nicole needs his help guiding her troubled son. Can they work together for a second chance at family?

———————

LICNM0823

Get 3 FREE REWARDS!

We'll send you 2 FREE Books plus a FREE Mystery Gift.

FREE
Value Over
$20

Both the **Love Inspired®** and **Love Inspired® Suspense** series feature compelling novels filled with inspirational romance, faith, forgiveness and hope.

HARLEQUIN
PLUS

Try the best multimedia subscription service for romance readers like you!

Read, Watch and Play.

Experience the easiest way to get the romance content you crave.

Start your **FREE TRIAL** at
<u>www.harlequinplus.com/freetrial</u>.